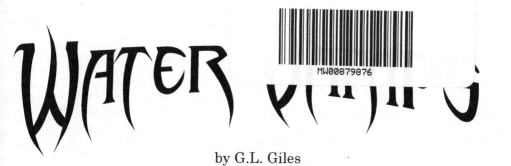

WATER VAMPS

by G.L. Giles

a BlackWyrm book
Louisville, Kentucky

WATER VAMPS

By G.L. Giles
Copyright ©2010, 2013 by G.L. Giles

All rights reserved, including the right to reproduce this book, or portion thereof, in any form. Written permission must be secured from the publisher to use or reproduce any part of this book, except for brief quotations in critical reviews or articles.

The characters in this novel are fictitious. Any resemblance to actual persons living or dead is purely coincidental.

A BlackWyrm Book
BlackWyrm Publishing
10307 Chimney Ridge Ct, Louisville, KY 40299

ISBN: 978-1-61318-147-8

Cover Artwork: Victor Sweatt

Second Edition: June 2013

Praise for G.L. Giles's "Water Vamps"

"Water Vamps is one of the most clever supernatural stories I've read in years... only the singular mind of G.L. Giles, in all her guile and wit, could have come up with the idea of aquatic vampires who behave like the sirens of yore. As wildly out to sea as the premise seems, Giles' rich, warm, and emotional writing style manages to make everyone seem so real, and our young protagonists, Robyn and Marion, are as grounded and substantive as can be. Water Vamps is a truly unique, engaging story – the sort of which makes G.L. Giles the worthy successor to the authors of my childhood (Ursula K. Le Guin, Madeleine L'Engle) and will certainly earn her a place in the canon of today's most imaginative and engaging emerging fantasy authors."

Staci Layne Wilson, *Dark Lullaby*, co-host of *Inside Horror*

"G. L. Giles once again brings vampires to life, this time in a young adult novel spanning centuries, dimensions and death. Giles' tale of protagonists Robyn and Marion includes all the usual suspects one expects from a good horror tale; vamps and werewolves, romance and loss, life and death. Mixing these ingredients with a brand new revisionist spin, Giles creates a world familiar yet astonishingly different from similar young adult fare. Giles has not forgotten what it is to be twelve. Armed with this knowledge, she lures readers in with interesting characters and daring messages not mired in traditional fantasy tropes. Giles cannily circles the familiar before transforming her tale into something entirely new. Water Vamps is a tale of tolerance and understanding, written in descriptive, engaging prose."

Will Colby, *KillingBoxx*

"G.L. Giles delivers a new concept to an old tale noteworthy of a fictional television documentary. Her descriptions of her characters lend charm and mystery to the history of how vampires have always been perceived. I think Stoker would be well pleased to see this 'new breed'."

Rena Short Brashear, Reviewer (for *Target Audience Magazine*, etc.)

"A good storyteller shows the 'human' in the alien creatures, in this case water vamps, and the 'alien' in the humans and G.L. Giles' "Water Vamps" lives up to a great fantasy tale because of it. A new kind of vampire is created in Water Vamps and Giles fascinates readers with those differences. It is not just blood sucking vamps but a kind of species that lives in water and behaves sometimes similarly to sirens. These creatures live by a set of rules – ones you probably haven't encountered before – and these codes are mirrored in the young lives of the human protagonists. Targeted for young adults, the depth of the story easily catches adult readers in its snare as all good fantasy/fairy tales do."

Gary Starta, Preditors and Editors Top Ten Science Fiction

"I was thrilled when I read about the Water Vamps that Giles created...every author needs to come up with a new twist that makes their vampires unique and memorable. With vampires seen as a species, Giles has definitely done this overall, but then she takes it a step further by creating an entirely new species that seems a little like a mermaid, a little like a siren, and all vampire!...Their story [is told in] "Water Vamps," and it will slake the thirst of anyone wanting to know more. Giles weaves a tale of intrigue and gives us a glimpse of the underwater world of the Water Vamps, and the history and origins behind these beautiful and dangerous creatures is truly unique!...We get to interact with these creatures on a more personal level: they go to school, have spelling and vocabulary tests, have to deal with their parents and even crush on each other. In this sense, we get to see the more 'human' side of the water vampires and see that the youth water vamps are similar to the human heroes, Robyn and Marion. Written for young adults, the main characters are children, and the adults are secondary to the story, which will appeal to any young adult. Robyn and Marion understand each other, and they (like the water vamps) have to deal with all the things children deal with, despite their unusual gifts. Even without these gifts, Robyn is a role model for any young female with her strength of character, respect for adults (at least those who deserve it) and her loyalty to Marion, who deserves his own credit for his loyalty and friendship...In the end, even the water vamps come to be [those] we can relate to and accept in this thrilling ride into the waters of Charleston, South Carolina."

Deanna Anderson for *Target Audience Magazine*

"G.L. Giles has written a YA book worthy of a closer look by young adults and adults of all ages. Her stories read like a welcome canteen of water when one has been in a desolate literary desert for too long. Let's face it. One can't throw a stake without hitting one of the many vampire novels out there these days. With Giles' book however, one hits a rich vein of gold or perhaps in this case, blood and, as every vampire knows, the life is in the blood. The life blood of "Water Vamps" is in the talent of such a gifted writer as Giles. Such are the literary riches one finds in "Water Vamps." If you love vampires, you are in for a rare treat. The most intriguing thing about her Water Vamps is that they are a fantastic and wholly unique twist on the vampire myth. Even if vampires are not your cup of tea (or goblet of blood) you will be engaged by Giles. It is her skillful writing style, engrossing narrative and some of the most interesting characters in all of literature that brings delight to the reader. I absolutely love the biracial storyline with Robyn and Marion. With this, Giles doesn't merely tell a story. She digs deeply into the human consciousness, bringing out old modes of thinking and revealing them in the light of day, inviting the reader to expand his or her mind. This is story-telling at its best. The most important thing I can say about this book is this: Best twist on the vampire mythos ever."

Evelyn Smith, *Transylvania, Louisiana*

"G.L. Giles creates a delightfully original vampire mythology in her young adult book Water Vamps. The main characters Robyn and Marion (aptly named after the literary adventurers Robin Hood and Maid Marian) engage in their own adventure involving Water Vampires, a complex hybrid of ravens and mermaids—with teeth! Giles celebrates the unconventional in numerous ways throughout the book, which any vampire-lover will embrace whole-heartedly. Her compelling tale follows the burgeoning young romance between Robyn and Marion which leads to their dangerous encounter with the Water Vamps. Giles mixes her unique history of vampires and the background of Charleston, South Carolina, creating a fully absorbing fantasy tale. Together, Robyn and Marion discover a pair of deceitful adults and a perilous, hungry species who are more than they appear to be on the surface and with whom they have more in common than they realize."

Bryce Warren, *Voodoo Mayhem*

PROLOGUE

November 2nd
(Day of the Dead)
Year Unknown
Ten Minutes Till Dawn
Somewhere Near the Carpathian Mountains

Setiana nearly lost her hooded cape in the heavy oak door that abruptly slammed behind her right after she crossed over the threshold and into the vestibule of sorts. She was thankful she'd been invited in by the grizzled old man, who was surprisingly spry for his advanced years, as he quickly bade her to advance inward with a wave of his wrinkled and sun-spotted hand. He'd anxiously peered behind Setiana and her companion to make sure they were alone before inviting them in. Both Setiana and her companion were well aware of what caused the thick wooden door to close so quickly, for they could both see and perceive the *Spirit Train of Dead Souls* that dwelled within the enclosed burial edifice they'd entered. Besides these intimidating spectral inhabitants, it was also laden with sarcophagi of various shapes and materials. Some made of marble, some made of stone and other materials, some with ornately carved designs–some with swans and some with ravens and other animals and many with angels–and some plain except for the inscriptions written on them, yet all of them beautiful, albeit it in a decidedly morbid way.

Setiana knew that she and her handsome companion had little time to get settled in for the day, so she looked up at her fellow traveler beseechingly. He was only two inches taller than she was, but he could feel her desperation, as she rapidly moved her eyes from his face to anxiously peer up at the round stained glass window about 100 feet above her on her left side somewhat past the grand foyer. The multi-colored panes were painstakingly placed in their soldered 'frames' and then collectively put in the large stone opening/window centuries before. It was unusual to have a grand stained glass window like that in the region then, but it was an atypical place all around, so it fit, strangely enough. It allowed only minimal light to illuminate the great dwelling of death, but even that small amount of light was dangerous to Setiana's kind.

Setiana hated the feeling of being at the mercy of the weathered human curator for her very existence, yet she certainly was. Even her loyal companion, Vasario, couldn't change that fact. Setiana knew that it would only take one direct ray of sunlight–hitting her through the stained glass somehow–for her to disintegrate into ashy vampiric remains. Vasario knew this fact very well, too, yet he tried to ease her discomfort and even partial despair by putting his arm around her lovingly. Sometimes, Setiana's despair was more pronounced, and she felt almost like letting a ray of sunlight touch her–just to end the agony of always having to be on the run. In contrast, Vasario would do everything in his power to ever keep that from happening! He loved Setiana too much to allow her to perish. She meant the world to him, and he proved his love for her daily.

The greedy curator knew their plight and desperation, as he was used to servicing their supernatural kinds. So, when Vasario shook out five gold coins from his pouch into the wizened palm of the old man–enough for the average person of the period to live off of for an entire month–he was surprised to see the curator grin wickedly and shake his head from left to right as a nonverbal cue that he was not taking the offer! The curator knew he had the upper hand, as his evil smile stretched further to reveal mostly rotted teeth with two of the more substantial ones housing a piece of fowl he'd eaten the night before between them. He moved his wrinkly fingers away from Vasario and toward his own body with a 'gimme more' signal. Vasario, realizing he had no choice with it being that close to dawn, if he wanted to save his dear Setiana, quickly emptied the rest of the contents of his pouch into the weathered, beckoning palm. He knew he'd always be able to replace gold coins, but never his most treasured: Setiana!

The old man had had to quickly cup one liver-spotted (from way too much sun-damage in his youth–part of the reason why the old man chose to now reside inside the enormous mausoleum) hand beneath his other to catch the great amount of clinking gold that had spilled from Vasario's pouch, but he did so quite nimbly, and, in fact, not a coin from the substantial mound dropped to the floor. Money was his dearest friend, so the elderly man made sure of that! Also indicative of the curator's rapid movement was the ecru-stained white gauze he had draped over his long-sleeve and right arm which had come to the aid of his greedy left palm. It fluttered like the desperate wings of a moth who'd gotten too close to a candle's light and was singed by it. Vasario looked at the gauze curiously, but he was too annoyed with the old man to ask why he carried it, and to ensure that no time was lost on retrieving coins should the elderly man drop them, he offered his pouch somewhat condescendingly with, "Here, take this, too!" The old man didn't have to be offered twice; he always took free gifts.

Vasario's main concern was to always keep Setiana safe at any cost–literally, in this case, and figuratively! He valued Setiana's existence above all others–including his own! He had gladly assumed his role as that of her guardian, as one of the select shape-shifting 'niners.' She being one of the remarkable 72 'setians.' Their co-existent bond was undeniable.

Though both Vasario and Setiana could have easily killed the offensive old man, they didn't for two reasons: they needed his knowledge of the mausoleum, and they weren't into taking lives over monetary disputes. In this outlook they were different from many 'niners' and 'setians,' who had absolutely no problem in taking the lives of what they considered to be 'lowly humans.' Vasario and Setiana were different; they had learned how precious ALL life is, and they were respectful of all forms of it, even if it were sometimes their supper. Both Vasario and Setiana had learned to drink from their prey without killing it. They only took what they needed to survive. A learned practice that most of their 'disrespectful' kinds didn't bother with.

Setiana and Vasario were at the mercy of the old inn-keeper of sorts due to their late check-in (with dawn fast approaching). They knew well the true stories of townspeople raiding tombs, etc. and decapitating vampires as they slept, so they put their faith in the curator to find a safe place (burial chamber) for Setiana for the day. The sarcophagi that ensured the most peace of mind for their resident vampires were the ones filled at the top level with the bones of humans who'd been dead for centuries. The locals (humans) felt no threat from them, as they were only concerned with the newly dead who they felt might easily arise from the dead to become vampires. And, while Setiana knew of this type of vampire, they weren't her kind. She had come into existence as a setian, not made a setian or a vampire, and some would consider that quite an honor.

"Hurry, hurry," the surprisingly spry old man said as he motioned for them to follow him. It wasn't so much that he cared for their survival, as it was that he was full of low-cunning and cared to have more gold coins cross his palms from them in the future—he considered repeat business a great thing! They quickly followed him from the foyer to another grand room and then another...then through a smaller room and then down some narrow stone steps. The quarried stone was originally white granite, but it had been sullied to various shades of brown by the soles of the desperate making their way to safety before the sun came up.

Before long, in one of the small rooms tucked off of the passageway at the bottom of the stairs, where they were, for all intents and purposes, *beneath* the main section of the mausoleum, the greedy 'innskeeper' showed his skill in finding Setiana the perfect 'room' for the day in his 'macabre hotel.' It was one of the oldest sections of the burial edifice with much of the newer parts of the somewhat sprawling mausoleum having been built on top of it. There were even a number of columbarium niches built into these ancient parts of the lower levels. People without the old curator's knowledge of the peculiar and somewhat haphazard layout had frequently become lost in it—especially in the sections of scattered catacombs beneath the mausoleum. And, many people had gone mad trying to find their way back due to the incessant aggravations at the same time by the spectral inhabitants who considered the mausoleum *their* home, so those humans who still held breath were, indeed, their unwanted visitors. So, many of the locals feared venturing into the section which would house Setiana that day—and this fact boded well for vampiric guests as a whole!

The safest sarcophagi for vampires, of most kinds, to sleep in were those whose inhabitants had been dead at least a couple of centuries. The townspeople felt no threat from them, as it was the newly dead who concerned them and/or the 'decidedly dead' (those who'd been vampires for years—like Setiana).

A beautiful marble headstone with a raven and a swan carved into it marked the top of the stone coffin where Setiana would sleep for the day. Its former inhabitant's bones still lay there, but her spirit had passed to her eternal life centuries before, so her spirit no longer haunted the mausoleum. Reaching into his sleeve, the same one with the gauze resting atop it, the old man retrieved a metal rod, about an arm's length in size, and used it to pry open the stone on top—much as one would use a crowbar. It slowly gave to reveal the old bones beneath. Then the old man quickly scooted the bones up and into the now unfolded gauze he carried, and then he tapped forcefully beneath where the bones had been lying just seconds before. Setiana and Vasario were amazed to see the bottom fold in from the sides to reveal where a cache of jewelry and coins used to be stored beneath. Many wealthy families chose to keep the family treasures of those who'd died buried this way, out of sight. It was to honor their dead, but to keep it away from grave robbers at the same time. This particular family had been unsuccessful in keeping their treasure hidden, as the curator had plundered it years ago.

Setiana, realizing this was to be her 'bed' for the day quickly jumped inside. The curator then placed his wrinkly 'pointer' finger inside the eye of the raven on the marble headstone...that closed the coffin 'bottom' again. Vasario made note of the taps to open and eye push to close—just in case the curator wasn't around next time.

The 'innskeeper' was then careful to take the bones from his gauze and lay them back on top of the coffin 'bottom'—above where Setiana was settling in for the day. She didn't have much room to move, but unfortunately she'd stayed in worse places during the day, so she tried to make the best of it. And, she gently whispered, "Forgive me," to the bones above her for disturbing their slumber, even though she could feel that the spirit had long since departed that collection of calcium. At any rate, Setiana didn't like being intrusive, so even though the spirit had gone, it made her feel better to whisper those heartfelt words.

Vasario even managed a weary smile when he saw the curator cover Setiana's hiding place with the skeletal remains and then close the heavy stone lid. The old man was going to lead Vasario to another adjoining 'cell' to slumper, as he incorrectly assumed that he was a vampire, too. However, Vasario quickly let him know differently with, "I'll be fine in here, too."

"Suit yourself," the curator, who could really care less, croaked. Waiting till the footfalls of the old man were just distant echoes, Vasario took in his surroundings further. There was a dim light emanating from the torch in a nearby hallway, but that was about it. Fortunately, he possessed the ability to see well in both the light and the dark, so it wasn't a problem for him.

Vasario took off his long, sepia-colored overcoat and laid it gently atop the closed stone coffin. As it turns out, there were going to be three 'coffin-guests' that particular night. He liked sleeping, or at least resting–he doubted he'd get any sleep there due to being ill-at-ease from the surroundings–in this manner to ensure that Setiana had even more protection should trouble arise–though he would be sure to vacate the top of that particular stone coffin if trouble did arise, as he would not want to tip anyone off to the fact that he was guarding something valuable, in this case Setiana, beneath. If somebody, besides the curator, or a group of people, etcetera came snooping around, then he'd know ahead of time with his heightened senses. Hopefully, the need would not arise, and they could both get some highly desired rest, but Vasario wasn't taking any chances when it came to his precious Setiana. That was the way of good guardians–especially if they were one of the 'niners.'

Though Vasario had adapted to the sleep-patterns which Setiana had no choice in, he did not have a problem with the sun's rays. In fact, quite the opposite was true: Vasario gained strength in the sunshine. Sometimes, when he couldn't sleep, and he felt that they were in a much safer locale than they were in that particular day–being in that enormous, relatively unguarded mausoleum–he'd shift into an animal of choice and run for hours in the sunlight till Setiana awoke. Like Setiana, however, he needed blood to survive, but he never drained his victims, be they human or animal, completely. In fact, some might argue that the 'victims' of his blood-thirsty survival were actually left off better than when he found them, as, in draining them, these 'victims' were left with a sense of peace, and they even acquired the ability to 'shift' their formerly negative thoughts into positive ones. Indeed, some of the people who Vasario'd drained had gone on to become great leaders, writers and such for their ability to afterwards contemplate issues in decidedly productive new ways. This resulted in much fame and fortune for many of those who'd been lucky enough to be Vasario's 'victims.'

Then there were those relatively rare times when their roles were temporarily reversed. Namely, during a full moon! It was then that Setiana would become the temporary 'guardian' of Vasario. So, about once a month, Setiana had to take care of Vasario who was unable to control his shape-shifting ability. He usually considered his ability to shift into many animals of choice a gift, but when he lost control during a full moon, his shape-shifting could be considered a liability. He was handicapped by his being a shape-shifter during this time because rather than having the ability to choose—like any other time—which animal he wanted to be, he was at the mercy of whatever animal he happened upon. So, if he came across a lion during the full moon, then he'd change into a lion. But, if he came across a mouse, then he'd change into a mouse. But, he had to be in fairly close proximity of the animal he'd unwittingly change into—about 20 yards apart or less. During the full moon, it was Setiana who kept Vasario close to guard *him*. Vasario could be near Setiana without turning into a vampire like herself—even during a full moon. In fact, she was one of the entities he could never change into. Their relationship was one of balance. His kind were commonly called the 'Niners,' but they were also known as the Horusians or the Therians to some. Many mistakenly thought that the Horusians and the Setians were mortal enemies, but in that they were quite wrong. Instead, they brought balance to their respective species and were guardians of each other—generally acknowledging their differences with respect and guardianship.

The last thing Setiana thought of before drifting off into her 'dead sleep' in the stone encasement was how grateful she was to have Vasario in her life. She was never truly lonely with him in it, and even though their very existence was certainly outside of 'normal' life, and it could be quite challenging always being on the lam in a sense, she loved him. They most certainly completed each other. And, she had to smile, with her fangs even bared briefly, when she thought of the first full moon they'd spent together. He'd gotten too close to a domesticated cat, and he had changed for a full 24-hours into a 'mouser.' Not only did he hunt and eat what cats eat as a cat, not sparing the animal's life as he usually would, but he also retained many of the cat's mannerisms even after changing back into his normal human-looking form. For example, he licked his hand to clean his face, etcetera, for a full week after changing back. While it caused him great embarrassment later on, it still served to amuse Setiana, and it only made him that much more endearing to her, as she loved cats. She longed to have some as pets, but it just wasn't possible with their nomadic lifestyle. She dreamed of settling down with Vasario, but she didn't see how that could happen anytime soon. They didn't have real roots anywhere but in Egypt. And, going back there was not a possibility—at least while others of their kind were still in existence. Setiana and Vasario hadn't exactly followed ALL the rules their kinds were supposed to, so they didn't exactly fit in with their former families in Egypt. It was a good day when Setiana dreamed of Vasario throughout her 'dead sleep'...other days, it wasn't as pleasant as she was sure she couldn't keep going existing the way they did with no permanent home. On the bad days she had nightmares during her 'dead sleep' in which she was being chased by angry humans carrying torches and wooden stakes.

'Dead sleep' was the time when vampires like Setiana revitalized their body. Once they entered it, then they were immobile till they awoke exactly 8 hours later. Generally, Setiana remembered nothing of her time in 'dead sleep,' but that day was different. She saw herself and Vasario in the woods holding hands, and then she saw what looked to be two human children, around 11 years old, just staring at them—these wise-looking children were also holding hands: the one, a lovely young girl with a dark complexion, and the other, a handsome young boy with blond hair. She and Vasario looked at the young couple lovingly, and the two young people (even though Setiana felt that they were still technically children, they had such wisdom about them, that many might take them for young adults) looked at them with curiosity. For a minute, it seemed as if the two couples were looking at each other through a looking glass. Then Setiana heard a voice echoing throughout her mind—even in the midst of her dead sleep continuously till she awoke with the words, *These counterparts can release you!* Setiana had no idea who was giving her the information, but she felt it to be true. On top of that, she realized that the children who could save her and Vasario from a hard existence, not really a life, on the run lived not only in a different place, but also in a different time! Much like in a fairy tale, though hers was more like a 'vampire tale,' the true love of these children for each other could break the miserable 'nomadic lifestyle spell' that Setiana and Vasario had rather inadvertently fallen into.

While Setiana was receiving all this new and hopeful information in her 'dead sleep,' Vasario had recently arisen from his rest, he'd sensed not to fall asleep in that place as it made him uneasy, to a state of being on high alert—not by the threat of humans for a change—by the disruptive presence of the *Spirit Train of Dead Souls*. This 'train' was formed by a bully spirit who forced other ghosts to attach their ectenic force, to all intents and purposes their ectoplasmic energy, to his own to make him a much more forceful entity. The 'engine' to this forced train was a malicious spirit known as Wilhelm (at any rate, it was his former 'human name'). He was known by many names by the other spirits, but all those were less than complimentary and always fear-based–names which human beings would have a hard time pronouncing, but they would have immediately evoked a feeling of dread upon hearing the malevolent and vicious sounds he was now named by the other spirits residing in the mausoleum. Even elsewhere in the spirit world, with those ghosts not attached to the mausoleum, the depraved nature of the one once known as Wilhelm was well known.

It was Wilhelm and his miserable spirit train of reluctant followers who'd been responsible for the heavy oak door to the mausoleum almost slamming shut on Setiana's hooded cape. And, as the old curator was a distant descendant of his, Wilhelm left him alone. However, the other humans, vampires and shape shifters who entered the mausoleum were fair game. *His game* to play with as he saw fit.

The poltergeist Wilhelm wasn't at all impressed by the fact that Vasario was a shape-shifter. He'd easily frightened both shape-shifters and vampires before, too! Easily terrifying humans was almost a given for Wilhelm and his reluctant 'railcars' crew. Of course, Wilhelm and his obedient followers wouldn't have understood this analogy, as railroads wouldn't even come into existence until centuries later. Wilhelm had been a ruthless bully when still human, and he unfortunately remained one in death.

Wilhelm loved shaking the stone coffins and other markers with the aid of his spectral following. The stone resting places sometimes shook so hard that their inhabitants' human remains were unsettled that way as well, so then they became the opposite of 'resting' places. Instead they became more along the lines of ruthlessly aggravated places. As Wilhelm and his poltergeist crew made their way to the sarcophagus housing Setiana for the day, Vasario looked him dead in the eye, with his arms crossed casually across his chest, and pointedly said to the bully Specter Wilhelm as he floated within five yards' propinquity, "Surely you don't mean to try and disturb my guardian's slumber."

"Surely YOU realize that I decide what or what doesn't happen around here," Specter Wilhelm hissed, causing a bundle of vomit-colored threads of energy to spew forth till they sickly dissipated into the air, while waving his ectoplasmic hands a few yards in front of Vasario's face menacingly.

"I realize that YOU are a bully who has absolutely no power over ME," Vasario retorted calmly, while at the same time emphasizing the words he wished to, even managing to smile at Specter Wilhelm at that point.

Furious that he wasn't eliciting the response of fear that his now spectral form fed off of, Wilhelm went around Vasario to the other side of the sarcophagus housing Setiana and slammed his no longer corporeal fist down on top of it. Even though his fist was no longer made of solid material, it still shook Setiana's resting place so intensely that even the headstone vibrated for some seconds afterwards. Concerned that his ward might awaken from her much needed 'dead sleep,' Vasario decided to take matters with Specter Wilhem and his ghostly group into his own hands–clearly the greedy curator wasn't going to step in and help (wherever he'd disappeared to after keeping his end of the 'stone coffin rental agreement' was unknown). By the looks of things, it seemed that Specter Wilhelm was the only real concern, not his ghostly followers, but Vasario was prepared to take them all on, if need be.

Right before Specter Wilhelm had a chance to repeat the action of slamming his fist down again atop the sarcophagus, Vasario started to change. But, strangely enough, it was not into another animal this time. No, it was something else. Something extremely bright! Vasario let the change take him over from the inside out, as he tilted back his head and opened his mouth widely. The light that had been emanating throughout his body in waves then coursed with direction to his neck and then pooled in his mouth before being shot from it in a dazzling arc of light. It took Vasario less than a second to then move his face level with Specter Wilhelm's face and release the direct ray of light into the malignant spirit's loosely bound face and form. It was seldom practiced by Horusians like Vasario, but if they were pure of heart like he was, then they had the power to harness the very sun in their body, and blast its rays at basically whomever they wanted. These sun's rays he'd harnessed and directed towards Specter Wilhelm ended up disintegrating the ghost for good. You see, the rays showed whomever they were directed at exactly who they truly were on the inside, and most were simply not able to handle the truth of their own existence–especially if they thought themselves superior to others as Wilhelm always had. As Specter

Wilhelm's form dissipated forever, the other spirits who'd followed him out of fear found themselves free at last–they no longer had to remain in a servitude 'train,' so many said goodbye to each other and spread to different sections of the mausoleum–some were even released enough to venture outside of it for the first time in centuries.

Fortunately for Setiana, who revitalized her vampiric body and mind with her daily 'dead sleeps,' she did not awaken with all that had transpired, and even more importantly, none of the 'harnessed sunshine' Vasario had used on Specter Wilhelm had seeped into the stone 'bed' where she was sleeping.

CHAPTER ONE
Robyn's Dream Meeting

November 3, 1985
(Robyn's 11th Birthday)
3 a.m.
(The Second Bewitching Hour)
Charleston, South Carolina
Nassau Street

Eleven-year old Robyn realized she must have already drifted off to sleep when she saw the bloody bandages steadily dripping globules of the red liquid from their positions on the ash trees. It is a special gift to be able to lucidly dream, aware that you're dreaming, but it made sense as Robyn was a very special child. In fact, she was naturally a lucid dreamer, and it might have had something to do with the fact that she was constantly questioning her reality. Even when awake! She tried not to be alarmed at her dream, she refused to even think of it as a nightmare, even when looking at the ghastly scene. And, it wasn't just the visual, for the atmosphere felt despondent as well. Robyn felt somehow that the bandages represented mental as well as physical wounds. Deep wounds. Age-old wounds, that she was somehow being called to heal. At first the forest with the ash trees felt desolate, as she saw not much more than them and the dripping bloody bandages. If Robyn had to describe the wooded area in one word, then *despair* would be the word. But fortunately she wasn't limited to just one word, so the more fitting description of them being *ridden with despair, but not completely full of despair* stuck in her head as she made her way through the forest. She could hear the whispers of spirits...their voices carried across the wind as she wound through the narrow paths between the ash trees. And, even though Robyn felt the pain of the forest and some of its ghostly inhabitants, she didn't let herself get bogged down in their sorrow. Rather, she was determined to make her way through there as quickly as possible and perhaps help them if she could.

One of the reasons Robyn was aware of her dream-state is that she was observing her dream-self from above, as kind of a third-party observer. Her conscious part, the real Robyn, was watching the dream-Robyn below, and in her experience—even at just 11 years old—that frequently meant a future path her conscious self would one day embark upon. A prophetic dream, of sorts. Though every aspect would not literally come to pass. It was more like an analogous representation of things to come.

So the real Robyn watched the dream-Robyn navigate through the ash trees for some time from above her. She thought it peculiar at first that dream-Robyn was wearing a Lincoln green outfit with a jaunty hat atop her head—with her long dark curls spilling down her back. Smiling broadly down at her dream-self, Robyn thought in her lucid dream, *Why, I look like a female version of Robin Hood!* Robyn had known for some time that Robin Hood had also been known as Robyn Hode, and she loved that they shared the same given name. They also had other traits in common. Robyn thought the love story between Robin Hood and Maid Marian one of the best ever recorded, as she admired loyalty and true love. Robyn wasn't sure she'd ever have such a *fortuitous* love in her life, as she'd never experienced anything even remotely like their love before—but she was just 11 years old! Besides, she identified more with Robin Hood than Maid Marian, so she didn't see how that would work out in a relationship.

The real Robyn's smile widened even more in her sleep, as she realized that her mother would have described her as having entered a function (dream) of the Astral Plane; that's why she could both be herself and see a version of herself at the same time. However, the real Robyn wasn't sure if she'd be able to control what took place in the dream or not.

At first, Robyn felt as if she were most likely still in South Carolina in her dream with the abundance of ash trees, and she even spied a few of the lovely large golden silk spiders as she made her way later on through the forest. Ash trees and golden silk spiders she'd grown up around all her life, so there was nothing strange in that. Fortunately, the ash trees she'd encountered in real life never had bloody bandages dripping off of them, however.

Robyn saw that the moonlight was shining down on the path her dream-self should take then—even though the vegetation was getting more and more dense. Plus, now there were other forest creatures afoot: wild cats, mice, snakes and such. The real Robyn wasn't afraid...just more curious now in seeing what would be revealed to her dream-self. As her dream-self continued to where the moonlit path was now leading her, it became more and more difficult to progress, as her path grew more narrow and the forest animals were becoming more and more riled up. Birds were now swooping dangerously close to her face, and one, a large raven, even knocked off her Robin Hood-green hat. Plus, more and more snakes appeared, the fast moving black racers, scurrying off her path and into the foliage only right before she put next foot down. Though the erratic behavior of the animals was unsettling, it wasn't nearly as creepy as the bloody bandages on the ash trees, so both the real Robyn and her dream-self kept their wits about them. The dream-Robyn ducked deftly beneath low-hanging Spanish moss (typical of the Lowcountry) and bravely stayed the course.

Somewhat concerned for her dream-self at that point, the real Robyn asked for protection for her. Almost immediately, lovely yellow Carolina Primroses (also known as Gladiolus) began lining her path. The dream-Robyn stopped for a few seconds to gather one of the wild-flowering and graceful Carolina Primroses in her hand. The next second she snapped it off of its stem and placed it behind her ear. It offset both the color of her cap and her long dark curls nicely. Quickly, the real Robyn thanked the faerie devas for their flowery gift in lieu of the dream-Robyn's thanks.

Robyn's mother, Leticia, had taught her years before that wearing a primrose aided in one's protection. So, the real Robyn was happy that her dream-self had the presence of mind to adorn herself with one, as she forged bravely onward. Suddenly it seemed, the dream-Robyn began shivering, and the real Robyn then saw the banana spiders' webs in front of her dream-figure now burdened with ice. And the real Robyn barely had time to utter to herself in her sleep, *That's strange,* before she noticed that it had begun to snow in her dream. Then it became abundantly clear that she was no longer in South Carolina, her home, as she heard piles of snow now crunching beneath her feet on the path. Then she looked down at her feet—the boots, a la Robin Hood, she was wearing making obvious tracks along the path. There was plenty of traction to keep her from slipping, and at first the snow was a beautiful powdery white.

The real Robyn marveled at the beauty of the snow falling on the path, as snow hardly ever fell in South Carolina. But then Robyn noticed that the snow beneath her dream-self's feet was less and less white in color. Even the air seemed murkier. The snow now looked defiled with dirt, or something else. It was unclear to Robyn exactly what the reason for the change in the dream's atmosphere was all about. But she had a feeling she would soon find out.

The tree branches were so dense as she continued on the path that just about when she was sure she'd no longer be able to go forward, she unexpectedly walked into a large clearing. The only things in the clearing besides herself were a monolithic stone monument of some sort and a sole camphor tree. As Robyn approached the monolith, she noticed that the stone looked centuries-old with many stains apparent and flagrantly streaking down it. And, it was curious that as she got closer to it, the colossal size it once seemed changed. It was definitely diminishing in size, and then even more strangely, it suddenly grew horizontally and lost much of its size vertically. She would have been completely absorbed in the visual change if it weren't for her olfactory perception becoming more and more stimulated as well. In fact, Robyn realized that the camphor tree (they were considered invasive in parts of the United States due to having spread out of control in some parts), though just a lone one in the clearing, was being invasive to her sense of smell. Even though the real Robyn's sense of smell was assaulted, via her dream-self, she really liked the smell of camphor. Plus, she remembered what her mother had told her about the camphor; it was used to help establish a bond between them and other practitioners and their Great Goddess! It was also used in overall healing. A very positive sign that the camphor tree was there, indeed!

Not as positive was what the monolithic structure had finally morphed into. Though much smaller in size now, Robyn could clearly see that it had become a rectangular-shaped stone sarcophagus. And, then her nostrils were assaulted again, but this time not by the pleasant camphor. Rather, they inhaled a disturbingly familiar iron-scent. Robyn couldn't put her finger on exactly what she was smelling at first, but she knew she'd come across it plenty of times...more around her mother than when alone. She racked her real brain in the dream world–trying to recall exactly what the scent was of– and then it dawned on her: Blood! And, the smell of the blood was growing increasingly stronger...she didn't even notice it much from the bloody bandages on the ash trees at the onset of her dream journey. Now, it was hard not to ignore it, as she noticed that the one camphor tree in the clearing had become laden with the bloody bandages. Robyn was sure that they weren't there before! Why now? She couldn't answer her own question, but she could observe.

She noticed visually then that the bandages on the camphor tree were dripping their blood much faster than the ones on the ash trees had. These bandages almost appearing to be wringing themselves out constantly with steady streams of blood falling to the ground and then forming into streams before running into the snow outside of the clearing. No wonder the snow looked so dirty. It had been sullied with blood!

The real Robyn shivered in horror for a second, but she was no coward, so she quickly decided to focus on something else to gather her wits about her. So, she and her dream-self turned their attention to the stone sarcophagus instead. Not that the stone sarcophagus was a whole lot less creepy than the excessive amounts of blood streaming into the forest. But, it was more stable-seeming, at least for the moment, as it had recently morphed from an upright monolith. The real Robyn felt the inclination to laugh (she had a way of coping with extreme fear in this manner), so she did, but it came out as a kind of snort from the dream-Robyn's mouth.

The next moment or so she felt compelled to move closer to the sarcophagus, so she did. Upon closer examination, she looked on in awe at the wonderful craftsmanship that had gone into the carving of the raven and swan which appeared on the marble headstone–which seemed to grow from either the stone coffin itself or the ground below just moments before. Robyn didn't really trust any of her senses completely in her dream world. But she did feel the urge to then trace her fingers along the outline of the raven and the swan stone carvings, so she did. It wasn't until she placed her pointer finger into the chiseled section of the raven's eye, however, that she became alarmed again. In fact, she almost immediately regretted her decision to have been so bold, for the heavy lid to the sarcophagus started to move back and forth before springing open. Robyn had discovered an ancient secret about how to open certain sarcophagi, one that many curators could have learned from to avoid having to use crowbars: the secret was that oftentimes one "eye" pushed in on the headstone triggered an opening mechanism.

Then dream events turned even stranger to the bewildered Robyn, as suddenly a lovely "woman" sprang out of the stone coffin. Robyn was mesmerized by her Amazonian-like beauty: she was tall, strong-looking, had long dark hair like Robyn's own but a much different complexion. Her face was a fine alabaster color and so was her neck, hands, arms, etcetera—every bit of her that was not clothed in fact. And, her clothes were quite out-of-the ordinary Robyn thought, though they looked like they'd cost a pretty penny. Old-fashioned was the first term that came to Robyn's mind, as she tried to process both the lady and her clothes quickly.

As quick-witted as Robyn was, she could not predict what would happen next. The fine lady seemed to almost float to right in front of her. And, then, not regarding an arguably healthy personal space stance, she lifted the dream Robyn's hands by placing her own palms beneath them. And, then she smiled down at Robyn offering, "My dear, you're so young, and yet, so able!" Not waiting for Robyn's dream-self to respond, she continued, but this time she didn't speak, rather she started to chant with a hauntingly beautiful melody coming from somewhere in the forest at the same time, "My blood is your blood, and your blood is my blood...we're one without sun...counterparts, though apart..." There was more to the song, but try as she might Robyn couldn't hear all of it clearly.

Though Robyn could no longer hear what the beautiful lady was saying, she could feel her good intent and powerful energy. Robyn felt so comfortable with her that she even beamed up at her at one point...until the lady smiled down at her, but this time she smiled with her fangs exposed. "Oh, my Goddess," Robyn gasped in disbelief. She knew that the lovely female vampire was not her Great Goddess, but she'd uttered the words as an expression of shock—even in her dream.

"Don't be afraid, My Dear," the female vampire responded soothingly. "You are like me, but a different kind of vampire."

"What?" Robyn managed, absolutely astounded at the transpiring dream events. "You must be mistaken. I'm Pagan, not a vampire."

At that the beautiful vampire, who was none other than Setiana, who'd crossed space and time to 'dream visit' Robyn, broke out in enticing peals of laughter which sounded like high-pitched bells of merriment. Even though Robyn saw that Setiana wore expensive clothing and carried herself with pride, she felt more at ease with her when she realized that she could be more down-to-earth as well, as evidenced by the genuineness conveyed in her laughter. When Setiana stopped laughing, she continued their conversation with, "Who's to say you couldn't be a vampire and be Pagan?" But, not wanting to confuse Robyn more, and realizing that her time was limited in Robyn's world, she seriously said, "You are a Psychic Vampire, Robyn."

"Even IF I were, then how would you know that?" Robyn retorted through her dream-self. She didn't like labels much, so she wasn't exactly welcoming Setiana's news.

"Because, My Dear, you're one of the 72 setians–incarnate as a human Psychic Vampire in this lifetime."

"But, how in the world would you know that–even if I were to believe you?" Robyn verbally volleyed back.

"You'll have to see if what I'm saying resonates with you," Setiana offered calmly. "I exist, for all intents and purposes, in a different place, time and even dimension than you, yet, I need you..."

"Why in the world would you need me?" Robyn interrupted.

"Because you need me. Think of me as one of your egregores, Robyn. But we're also more than that because we share the same bloodline, but yours is very diluted and it has mutated into human form."

"I do not understand," Robyn replied softly.

"How could you?!" Setiana responded compassionately. "I barely understand myself. It's just that I have already realized that we need each other."

"But how could I possibly help you?" Robyn queried again, desperately trying to grasp what was being told to her.

"Now we're getting somewhere," Setiana spoke softly. "It has to do with love."

"Love?" Robyn asked incredulously.

"Yes, love," Setiana said, matter-of-factly.

"Well, love for whom then?" Robyn countered, finally feeling like she might be able to get a more firm grasp on the content of her dream.

"My Dear, you are intuitive," Setiana replied, proud of her girl counterpart's quick processing. Then she added, "Kind of like the kind of love you'd feel for a boyfriend."

"A boyfriend?" Robyn queried with disbelief. "You do know I'm 11 years old, right? Most kids my age don't have BOYFRIENDS. Friends who are boys, sure, but boyfriends?! I think you may be barking up the wrong bloody camphor tree, Lady." The thought that the lady might be 'barking mad' Robyn kept to herself. She didn't think it in her best interests to be rude to a vampire!

"You will meet him soon," Setiana replied with a knowing smile. "And, you can call me Setiana–not Lady."

Slightly embarrassed that Setiana must have heard even her dream thoughts, Robyn retaliated with, "Okay, well even if I do and that somehow helps you, then how will you be helping me?"

"Good question, My Dear, and the answer is simple: I am your Guardian."

"Look, I don't mean to be rude," Robyn's dream-self said while the real Robyn looked on from above, "but I really don't see HOW a VAMPIRE can help me, as I'm a VEGETARIAN!"

At that Setiana spontaneously erupted into louder rings of laughter, but managed to stop for a few seconds to say, "That's rich, My Dear, yes, you're a vegetarian, and I'd never ask you to get my meals for me. I will help you in other ways."

"Well, today is my birthday," Robyn offered, surprised that her dream-self had actually said it aloud, versus just thinking it.

"Well, not exactly what I meant," Setiana responded, before the real Robyn saw the scene before her start to disintegrate, as she was being pulled from the dreamscape back into the 'real' world. "Not much time now, My Dear...I see...don't worry...you'll be getting your PUPPY as a present sometime today..."

"My PUPPY?" Robyn questioned. That makes no sense at all. My mother won't allow us to have a puppy right now. Things haven't been the best for us financially.

"Your PUPPY!" Setiana stressed, before disappearing completely. Moments later, Robyn was sitting up in her bed–fully awake!

Dismissing the dream as just that, Robyn stretched, got out of bed, walked to her closet and began sorting through clothes–green was her favorite color, so she had a plethora of clothes in that color to choose from. And, she wanted her 11th birthday outfit to be extra special.

CHAPTER TWO

The Gift

Robyn's neighborhood was built long before cars ever made their appearance; the narrow streets were built in a time that horses labored in front of and tied to the carriages that carried the wealthy people of the time, who kept them as their own—regardless of how the horses themselves felt about it. So, in the mid-1980s, on the day of Robyn's 11th birthday, Nassau Street, where she lived, was already crowded with the cars, trucks and vans of the residents who frequently found it challenging to even park all their own vehicles. So, many of Robyn's birthday party guests were already running late due to having to park blocks away—the only places they could find parking spots available without illegally parking on yellow lines and getting ticketed or, worse yet, towed, if they parked in the handicapped parking spots.

Robyn and her mother were glad that their guests were running late because it had taken longer than they'd figured on to get the lime green dress which Robyn had chosen laced up her back. She had matching green tights on, as November in Charleston, South Carolina could get a bit chilly, with a jaunty chartreuse-colored hat with a faux feather attached under a thick band which ran around the circumference of the felt (the synthetic fibers—not wool—kind) hat. Pleather, Robyn refused to wear leather, yellowish-green ankle length boots completed her outfit.

If Robyn and her single-parent family were church-goers, then her outfit would have been perfect for the local churches, but they were not—by choice. Robyn grew up under the caring tutelage of her mother, Leticia Lucas, with her extensive knowledge of many Gullah traditions and their ways mixed with Romani (ethnicity) ways. Leticia Lucas was, indeed, a very wise woman, and she was also a benevolent mother and friend. Though her bloodlines were Gullah and Romani, she decided upon the Disciplined Eclectic

Pagan route in raising her own children. With the ever-important caveat being known that they were always free to choose their own religion or none– at any age–in her house.

As most of her friends were still Christian in the Bible Belt, Robyn had gone to many Christian churches to check them out– since her mother was open-minded enough to encourage her to experience, think and ultimately choose for herself. While Robyn found many of the ecumenically-inclined churches tolerable, none of them were for her, as she found Christianity as a whole too male-dominated. She knew about the Father, and the Son and the Holy Spirit as the trinity, but she preferred her Holy Trinity to be the three aspects of her Great Goddess: maiden, mother and crone. Plus, Robyn believed in the doctrine of *Live and let live,* so while she was proud to be an Eclectic Pagan, she didn't care how anybody else chose to live.

After making sure that Robyn was properly laced up, she'd already spent a lot of time helping Robyn curl her long ebony hair into soft ringlets, Leticia became focused on her task of placing flowers (namely, her Roman roses) in crystal vases around the house. The last Roman rose she was dealing with, from her own garden in the back yard, was intent on giving her a hard time before it was to be set alongside the other Roman roses–amidst some beautiful white flowering Gypsophilia (also known as baby's breath)–in her most cherished sterling silver vase: a wedding gift from her former in-laws. This difficult rose had some particularly pronounced thorns growing on all sides of its stem. And, Leticia was being somewhat careless in her handling of it.

Robyn smelled the iron in her mother's blood before she saw it. And, she was almost immediately taken back to the bizarre dream she'd had. The one where she was in the forest with the bloody bandages...and a vampire! Yet, she'd smelled the strong iron-smell, frequently indicative of blood, around just her mother in real life before, too. *But, my mom's not a vampire, right?* Robyn mused.

"Darlin', be a love and get me a bandage, would you?" Leticia asked, snapping Robyn out of her disturbing thought. "A thorn got me again." And, the moment Robyn turned from her mother to fetch her a bandage and ointment, Leticia started nursing on the blood freely flowing from her wounded thumb. She knew that it disturbed her daughter to see her feed on her wounds this way, so she had waited till Robyn left the area. Leticia's practice of

autovampirism wasn't exactly birthday party material either, so she quickly drew as much blood as she could from her own thorn-pricked wound, by puckering her lips and inhaling in quickly her own sticky substance/lifeforce, for maximum sucking in/ingesting, right up till she saw Robyn returning with the items to help her mother heal. Leticia did not want to let her daughter know that she was, indeed, a certain kind of vampire, too. Her kind were frequently known as sanguinarians. And, not all of them were as kind as Leticia, for most fed on other people and animals, not on themselves.

"Here, mom," Robyn said, quickly putting some ointment on the padded part of the bandage and wrapping it around her mother's thumb. And, looking up at her mother with concern, she added, "Hey, why don't you let me arrange the flowers next time?"

"Darlin', you're more than welcome to help me anytime you'd like," Leticia responded. Somehow Robyn didn't believe she meant it, though. Strangely enough, Leticia had more energy after ingesting her own blood somehow, even though autovampirism wasn't supposed to work that way since she'd just taken in her own life-force again through her own blood, but Leticia wasn't just any ordinary human being, so maybe that was why. She was a sanguinarian-human, but, perhaps even more importantly, also a loving witch. However it worked, Leticia felt a burst of energy after drinking even just that small amount of her own blood, so she had the house up to her party specifications in no time after that. It was as if she'd just had a whole pot of coffee to herself.

Robyn couldn't help but notice her mother's increased activity, and, quite frankly, it made her stomach roil, knowing the reason for it, but there was nothing she knew to do about it. *Hey, maybe that vampire in my dream would know what to do about it...didn't she tell me she was my Guardian, or something...would that mean letting me know how to help my mother–since I need my mother around for a long time? Anyway, who am I foolin'...it was just a strange dream that...what was her name again?...oh yeah, some figment of my imagination named Setiana appeared in.* Still, Robyn couldn't help wonder more about the dream meeting. Not only had it seemed very real, but she wasn't entirely convinced that her 11-year old brain had it in it to dream up a scenario like that. The frustrating thing was, as in the situation with her mother, too, she had absolutely no idea how to go about handling either of the out-of-the-ordinary happenings. So, she decided to just go on as optimistically as was possible under the circumstances. Plus, if she didn't get a puppy–like Setiana said she would–for her birthday, then she fully intended to dismiss the dream meeting completely.

Unfortunately, Robyn's least favorite family member, Uncle Jonas, arrived first. With purpose, he kicked the welcome mat to the side before entering. Many would have thought his doing so rude, but Robyn knew it was to disturb the brick dust carefully placed underneath it. Brick dust was known to keep out unwanted spirits and haunts, like haints, and with Uncle Jonas being Robyn's uncle–and blood brother to her mother, Leticia–it was strange that knowing that, he'd put his own blood in danger, but if anyone really knew Uncle Jonas, as Robyn and her baby brother, Little Sean, did, intuitively–that is Uncle Jonas's true nature, then they'd have known he was certainly up to no good. He'd hated every member of his old elementary family–of which Leticia was a part. In fact, he hated most everyone, including himself, as he'd sadly chosen hate as a whole over love long ago. He was a truly miserable person, and he wanted everyone else to be, too. He certainly lived up to the hackneyed expression: Misery likes company. Add to that, he was insecure, so he wanted to make sure those closest to him would always remain dependent on him.

Uncle Jonas was Leticia's brother, but besides the fact that they both had black skin, there was little they had in common. While Leticia had big, empathetically-expressive doe-eyes (she kept her innocent wonder of the world, even though she was extremely knowledgeable), Jonas had small, squinty and beady-eyes. His small eyes reflected his narrow and fearful outlook on life. And, Leticia valued education, but Jonas didn't, for yet another thing. Obviously, she also took human welfare more to heart than he did. Plus, Leticia was a proponent of the Old Ways being a Practicing Pagan whereas Jonas had chosen to be a Fundamentalist Christian, much to the dismay of his former nuclear family. But, they believed in *Live and let live*, so they still accepted him, regardless of his religious choice. Also, except for the fact, perhaps, that she ingested her own blood, Leticia was a vegetarian like her daughter, Robyn. Whereas Jonas was mostly a carnivore, eating vegetables only on rare occasions. And, he never ate fruit. Jonas ate so much meat that his body was basically a walking graveyard. Many had commented on his revulsive scent, and Robyn knew it to be the smell of death seeping out of his pores. There was some Christian bible passage that Uncle Jonas always quoted, but Robyn refused to acknowledge by learning it...something like animals were put on the earth to be the servants of mankind, to use them in whatever manner they liked– including killing and eating them. The notion was simply barbaric to Robyn and her refined mother. Robyn certainly didn't agree with 'animal slavery,' or any other kind of slavery for that matter.

"Come in," Robyn said, in invitation to her unseemly, in both appearance and action, uncle.

"H-h-here's your present," Jonas said, handing the poorly wrapped gift to Robyn as he stepped over the threshold. He frequently stuttered, and it caused many to take pity on him when they really shouldn't have, as it only served to help him use his disability as a crutch.

"Thanks," Robyn offered, but then quickly turned her fashionable '80s boots to leave him standing there in order to place his present on the old oak table her mother had set up for presents in the center of the room which was well-lit with natural light from the impressive bay windows. Besides, she didn't like to stay around him and his draining energy for too long. His wife's draining presence was even worse! But, Vanna Dittmar (she was really Vanna Dittmar Lucas after marrying Jonas Lucas, but she refused to go by anything but the name she was raised as: Vanna Dittmar) couldn't make it to Robyn's party, as she was too busy running their shipping store in Summerville, South Carolina. Robyn had breathed a huge sigh of relief when she'd learned that Vanna Dittmar wasn't coming.

Robyn was in no hurry to open Uncle Jonas and Aunt Vanna Dittmar's gift, as they were known for giving oftentimes shoddy or used and re-gifted ones. Always inappropriate for whomever was the recipient, too. Last year, Robyn had received a KJV bible from them, even though she'd told them that she wasn't Christian, but that didn't stop them from always trying to convert her. She and her mother just donated it, as it wasn't much of a 'present' to them. She had no idea what her 'present' from them was that year, but she'd lay money on the fact that it would soon be donated, too.

Anyone who spent too much time around either Vanna Dittmar or her husband, Jonas Lucas, usually felt incredibly drained afterwards. And, in rare cases, even suicidal. Their shipping shop in Summerville was a hotbed for malicious gossip, and Robyn could almost swear that Vanna Dittmar was draining off of the negative energy it/she stirred up. Vanna Dittmar's husband, Uncle Jonas, loved stirring the gossip pot, too; he always felt better when he could point the finger away from himself and onto others.

As Robyn walked away from the 'birthday gift table,' she had an epiphany of sorts: *What if her heinous uncle and aunt (Jonas and Vanna Dittmar) were...what did the Vampire Setiana refer to her as? Oh yeah, a Psychic Vampire...well, what if Vanna Dittmar and Jonas were Psychic Vampires, too? But, instead of being the ethical sort, like Robyn realized she might be, they were the horrible only-draining (never-giving back) sort? It would certainly explain a lot of things. Living in a family of human vampires! Not the fictional kind, but the real kind that fiction was patterned after.*

Robyn didn't have a chance to contemplate it further, as kids from her neighborhood started pouring in, and within minutes she was happily chatting and laughing with many of them. Robyn made a point of keeping her distance from Uncle Jonas whenever possible, but she noticed with much chagrin that he'd already cornered her poor mother in conversation a few minutes later. She could almost see the energy leaving her mother's body and getting absorbed into his, as he drained her with his negativity. Robyn wished her mother would simply cut ties with her brother and his wife, Vanna Dittmar. She didn't understand foolish loyalty like that, but she was just a child, and it was her mother's choice and not her own.

Leticia Lucas had lots of wonderful vegetarian fare spread out on her sideboard to the left of the 'birthday present table' and against the wall. There was a large platter of 'veggie burgers,' condiments, birthday cupcakes and cake pops (Leticia had been making them since the early '80s—well before they became mainstream popular). Robyn fully intended to make her way to her own 'birthday spread' soon, but she was interrupted in her quest for the great 'veggie fare' by Uncle Jonas' actions: targeting her mother to drain energy from was one thing, but now he'd set his sights on draining Sean, Robyn's three-year old baby brother! And, Robyn wasn't about to let that happen. Draining from an adult was one thing, but from a baby?! Robyn immediately started going towards Sean's playpen. Surprisingly, she made it there before Uncle Jonas.

Jonas was surprised at how quickly Robyn had moved to the playpen. In mere moments, she'd travelled across the room—clear to the other side—and quickly scooped up her baby brother into her arms. Sean looked up at her beaming—with a precious smile that revealed some of his baby teeth. Though she'd seen what Uncle Jonas was about to do by where he was heading, something else had tipped her off first, unbeknownst to her consciously: it was Baby Sean beckoning to her mentally which had really made her aware of his plight.

Robyn and her baby brother, Sean, had had this uncanny connection for as long as she could remember. They would often communicate telepathically. As Sean was just three years old, he didn't know very many words, but he could easily relay his feelings to his older sister. She'd sometimes see what Sean telling her in her mind, as a large picture of something. For instance, when he was hungry, he'd send her a vision of his baby food. Like Robyn and their mother, Leticia, Baby Sean was a vegetarian. And, long before many mothers knew about the benefits of organic baby food, Leticia was serving him many vegetables, with no pesticides, grown right in her garden. And, Baby Sean loved them!

Though Leticia swore to Robyn that she hadn't named her son after Little John, one of Robin Hood's Merry Men (second-in-command to Robin Hood, in fact—or, perhaps, in mythology), being that Sean is the word for John—Sean being from Irish origins. Little John...Baby Sean...too coincidental Robyn thought, especially since her name was Robyn. Either that, or it was some kind of cosmic joke—albeit a benevolent one. There could have also been a third possibility, too: that Leticia named him Sean after Little John subconsciously, and her conscious mind simply refused to admit it.

Regardless of their names, Robyn and her brother, Baby Sean, were very close siblings, and that made their mother so proud. There was no petty jealousy, as is oftentimes the case with siblings—many times spurred on to compete with their own blood due to their parents' insecurities. Leticia was an exemplary mother in many ways, and one of the ways it showed was in how her children related to each other.

"H-h-hey, why d-d-id you do th-th-at?" Uncle Jonas asked Robyn. He was clearly annoyed that Robyn had blocked him from being able to drain the innocent energy of Baby Sean.

To keep him out of your clutches, you no-good excuse for an uncle! Robyn wanted to say to her Uncle Jonas. However, she wisely guarded her words and responded with, "Sean gets scared when lots of people are in the house. He's only comforted if either me or mom picks him up at times like these." It was a lie, for sure, but it was the best excuse that Robyn could come up with to keep her brother safely out of the reach of their uncle. Then Jonas shook his head as if he weren't buying the story, and both Robyn and Sean knew what they had to do. Looking down knowingly at Sean in her arms, the two locked both eyes and thoughts. Together, Robyn and Sean started scrambling Jonas' thoughts. Their Uncle Jonas became disoriented, and he forgot what he'd been doing or even saying for the last few minutes. Acting like she was helping her Uncle Jonas, Robyn quickly put Baby Sean back in his playpen. Then she glanced back at her baby brother with a look which conveyed that she had Uncle Jonas under control now. And, indeed, she did! She guided Uncle Jonas to the vegetarian spread, and she told him to eat, as she knew he loved 'veggie' food; which, of course, he did not. However, her mental sway was considerable, and when combined with that of her brother, it was truly amazing to behold!

Robyn stared in wonder at her uncle basically doing her and Baby Sean's bidding. *Maybe that strange Vampire Lady...Setiana...from my dream was right...maybe I am a Psychic Vampire...then is Baby Sean one, too? Can vampires really be vegetarians because I know for sure that Sean and I are vegetarians?!* Before Robyn had an opportunity to contemplate her own thoughts more, their doorbell rang. Robyn thought it strange, as she was sure that all her party guests had already arrived. She headed for the door after passing by her birthday present table of well-wrapped gifts, with the exception of the one Uncle Jonas had brought, and she couldn't help thinking, *Well, MAYBE Setiana was right about me being a certain type of vampire, what she called a Psychic Vampire, but she was certainly wrong about me getting a puppy for a birthday present!*

As it turns out, Leticia beat Robyn to the door. Robyn was constantly amazed that her mother could move as quickly as she could, perhaps even faster if she'd recently ingested some of her own blood. Leticia swung the door open to face one of the most handsome men she'd ever laid eyes on. In fact, he reminded her of her children's father, with his blond hair, sculpted jawline and ocean-blue eyes. Especially since his countenance was kind, as her deceased husband's had been. Her husband's last name was Lucas, too, so it was kind of funny to know that Leticia was technically

Leticia Lucas Lucas, but she generally just went by Leticia Lucas. It was more common in Charleston Society than many from the outside might think—marrying someone with the same surname. The man at her door took her breath away slightly, but she tried not to be obvious about it, as Robyn had joined her at their threshold, and she didn't want Robyn to see her reaction to the good-looking stranger. Leticia didn't have to worry, as Robyn was more taken with the brand new 1985 Mercedes which was parked illegally in front of the long yellow line where their driveway led to their fence. People weren't supposed to ever park there since they'd be blocking the driveway, but Robyn could already tell that this man was so charming he could get away with just about anything. And, she was correct. However, what she didn't realize yet is that the super-attractive man chose to be ethical much more often than not, and that was a rare thing—especially with business dealings in the '80s!

Robyn's heart skipped a beat when she thought that maybe the stranger was no stranger at all, but, rather, someone from her daddy's side of the family. They weren't close to that side of the family, so it was a possibility…but her hopes of that diminished by the second, as she heard the man introduce himself to her mother with an outstretched hand and, "Good afternoon, my name is Andrew Simons."

"Is that a Simons with one 'm' or two 'ms'?" Leticia asked, surprised that the words had escaped her lips, as she wouldn't have felt comfortable enough to ask many strangers about their surname. Though much emphasis was still put on surnames in Charlestonian society, outright asking, though admirable to some who were bold and progressive, was considered a bit too forward. Much knowledge was imparted behind closed doors still.

"Definitely a Simons with one 'm,'" Andrew Simons, who was only growing more appealing to both Leticia and Robyn by the minute, said with a wink. You see, in Charleston, South Carolina, it was a fairly well-known fact, at least in the circles in which Leticia and Robyn interacted, that the one 'm' Simons had the reputation of being a lot more liberal than the two 'm' Simmons. For example, many one 'm' Simons were champions for gay rights long before it was more accepted in mainstream society, and many were proponents of biracial marriages long before it was common— like the marriage which had lovingly taken place between Leticia and Robyn and Sean's father—etcetera.

"Leticia Lucas, nice to meet you, and this is my daughter, Robyn. You'll have to excuse the noise inside, as it's Robyn's 11ᵗʰ birthday today!"

"Happy birthday! My son's just about your age. In fact, his birthday was just a week ago today," Andrew offered, glancing over at his new Mercedes. "As a matter-of-fact, he's here now...in the car."

Not forgetting her manners, Leticia graciously said, "He's welcome to come in for cake and food, if he'd like."

"I think he'd like that...let me ask him to be sure," Andrew said, agilely hopping down a few of their stone steps. But then he turned back unexpectedly and quite quickly, as if he'd just thought of something important, to look up at Leticia, shielded his eyes with his right hand in the bright sunshine, and added, "By the way, I'm here because I'm a real estate agent. I have been canvasing the area to see if anyone was interested in having their house listed by me. Real estate prices are going up around here...this neighborhood is majorly on the rise—lots of Charlestonian movers and shakers taking notice of it." Normally, Leticia would have been turned off by his type: Salespeople. But something in his demeanor felt sincere. For one thing, he'd been honest about his intent before entering her house, and she appreciated that. For another, he was certainly easy on the eyes.

"Real estate agent, huh?" Leticia said with a smile, "Well, you're *still* welcome in our house."

Within minutes, Andrew and his son were in their house. Robyn wasn't too disappointed in the fact, either, as Andrew's son had a winning smile and just the right amount of shyness when addressing her with, "Hey, I'm Marion...Marion Simons...sorry to disrupt your birthday party and all."

"It's no problem," Robyn responded. "Where do you go to school?"

"Porter Gaud, and you?"

"Our mom is home schooling us."

"Really?! I'd love to not have to go to school. Stay home and study or follow my dad around all day."

Robyn was surprised at his reaction, as most of the time when she told other kids about it, they immediately thought her weird. Almost as if she had a sickness they could catch. "It's okay, but I miss being around more people my age. I mean, there are some in this neighborhood, most of them being here at my party, but not a whole lot–really."

"Well, even though I go to a private school, it can be rough. I mean, I had to deal with bullies saying I had a girl's name for the longest time," Marion offered.

"It is an unusual name for a boy to have," Robyn began, and then quickly added, "but I happen to like many things out of the ordinary."

"Yeah?! Well, me, too, and I actually like my name because of whom I'm named after."

"Really?! Who's that?"

"Well, you may know him as the Swamp Fox. But his real name was Francis Marion. He was my ancestor. My full name is: Francis Marion Simons. I could have gone by Francis, but I'd still have been bullied for that name, too–I think."

"Yeah, I suppose–by those possessing ignorant minds," Robyn said with a smile.

"Right," Marion said in agreement.

"I remember studying a little about Francis Marion when we were studying South Carolina history," Robyn added, keeping their conversation going. "He's actually one of the few people of that time period whom I did like. I remember reading about him utilizing early guerilla warfare tactics–and hiding out for long periods with his men in the swamps."

"Yep," Marion answered, surprised that a girl would have remembered about guerilla warfare tactics. It made him even more attracted to her. So he suddenly said, "But, hey, enough about me...what about you? I don't even know your name."

"Robyn," she said simply.

"Okay, Robyn. Well, thanks again for letting me and my dad crash your party." Nothing was said of the fact that their names were Robyn and Marion. And, nothing was brought up about Robin Hood and Maid Marian. In fact, they both remained speechless after that till they were interrupted by Uncle Jonas's departure. He looked dazed and confused, as he strode past them without so much as a goodbye to Robyn and headed for the street, not even remembering for a second where he'd parked his car on it.

"Now that's a strange guy," Marion offered.

"Yeah, gotta agree with you there...and unfortunately, he's my uncle."

"I'm sorry...I didn't mean to insult someone in your family."

"Well, you did, but you didn't insult ME," Robyn laughed. "Between you and me, I know he's my uncle and all, but I don't like him."

"I can see why...rude, much?! Not even telling you goodbye and brushing right past us."

"Yeah, he's rude alright, but I was happy not to have to deal with him anymore today. But, hey, enough about my Uncle Jonas...you wanna go have some cake?" And, at that they both laughed, as they realized they'd been standing inside the house, true, but only just over the threshold for the last 30 minutes or so.

Marion couldn't believe how at home he felt when minutes later Leticia gathered everyone around her daughter, and they all sang the "Happy Birthday" song to her. Marion glanced over at his dad, and he could see that he was feeling much the same. They hadn't felt that way since...since his mom had passed over two years ago. It was a good feeling, and neither Marion or his dad wanted it to end. But they were kinda uninvited guests to Robyn's birthday party, and they didn't want to overstay their welcome either.

"Look, I certainly appreciate your inviting us into your home like this," Andrew said to Leticia, while taking his dish to the sink. "And, if you're ever looking to sell, then here's my card."

"Sure thing, thanks for the offer," Leticia acknowledged, by tucking the card into her khaki pants' pocket.

Seeing his father was saying goodbye, Marion turned to Robyn and spurted, "Look, I'm so sorry I didn't get you a gift."

"Well, wasn't your birthday just a week ago?" Robyn questioned.

"Well, yeah, but..."

"Well, I didn't get you a gift either," Robyn said with a smile.

"But you didn't crash my birthday party either."

"True, but you made it more fun, so I'm glad you showed up...Marion." Something in the way she said his name made Marion flushed, so he quickly followed his father outside to not reveal it, if possible. But by the time Marion was outside, his father was already in their new car, so he bounded down the stairs—much as an excited puppy dog would.

About that time, Leticia joined her daughter in the doorway, and putting her arm around her daughter's waist, she exclaimed, "Great Goddess, that boy has a lot of energy! Reminds me of a rambunctious puppy dog!"

"What did you say, mom?" Robyn asked, not exactly believing her ears.

"I said Great Goddess..."

"No, not that part, mom," Robyn uncharacteristically interrupted. "The last part."

"I said he reminds me of a rambunctious puppy dog!"

"Right, mom" Robyn agreed, and then she considered her words slowly before saying, "I got a *puppy* for my birthday."

CHAPTER THREE

Marion's Dream Meeting

October 27, 1986
(Marion's 12th Birthday)
12 a.m.
The First Bewitching Hour
Murray Boulevard
Charleston, South Carolina

Marion wasn't sure he was dreaming at first because he wasn't familiar with lucid dreaming like Robyn was. It certainly felt real at first because he could even smell the pluff mud and watch as fiddler crabs, also known as calling crabs, scurried before him in the swampy area, typical of parts of the Lowcountry. He had imagined his great ancestor, Francis Marion (the Swamp Fox), trudging through the pluff mud and saltwater with his men many a time. Tight-fitting boots in the pluff, sometimes referred to as plough, mud were practically a prerequisite, as it was easy to sink into this strange mixture of mud in the salt marsh. If that happened, then one could easily get cut on the oysters growing there. Mosquitos also thrived in the marsh along with ample spartina grass. Marion knew that the distinctive pluff mud smell, that many who hadn't been raised in the area found particularly offensive, was the result of decomposing plants and animals, as well as that of organic fecal matter and clay. In short, it was a detrivore's dream spot: the salty marsh areas of the Lowcountry.

Not that Marion minded the pluff mud scent, as he was born and raised in the Lowcountry and had grown accustomed to it, but he was quite pleasantly surprised by what he experienced olfactory-wise next. It was then that Marion realized he must be dreaming, as the landscapes had changed so quickly, and he actually used one of the words he'd had to define on a vocabulary test at Porter Gaud the previous week. He realized that he wouldn't use a word like 'olfactory' in his awake hours unless he was at school, and judging by the swampy scene he'd just been in and the wonderful landscape he was now in, he clearly wasn't at school. Unless it were the coolest school ever–Mother Nature's School!

In this new dream landscape, Marion could see and smell the wonderfully fragrant tea olive trees, which were also abundant in South Carolina, and he could see and hear the spiky sweetgum pods (also known as witches burrs) crunching beneath his feet. He could feel the sun shining down on him, and he could see the blue Carolina sky spread above him for miles it seemed.

However, that pleasant scenery didn't last long, as he could smell the next place before he actually saw it. Instead of smelling the sweet delicate fragrance of the tea olive trees' small white flowers, he smelled something which reminded him of the multi-vitamins he took daily at his father's prompting. To be exact, he smelled iron. It was unmistakable now. The scent of iron in blood! And, before he even realized that the ground had changed, his boots which were perfect for walking in pluff mud began slipping on the icy snow. Clearly he, like Dorothy Gale from *The Wizard of Oz* movie when she was no longer in Kansas, wasn't in South Carolina anymore!

Right about the time Marion was about to take a nasty tumble onto the snow, which would have surely changed his dream into a nightmare, he caught himself on the branches of a camphor tree with his outstretched arms and hands. Clinging to the branches stopped a nasty fall, but he was grossed out by what he'd inadvertently grabbed at the same time. Some kind of bloody bandage had evidently been on one of the tree branches, and now it was pressed into his right hand. Gaining his balance more on the icy snow, by planting his feet about shoulder-width apart and digging his heels in, he managed to stand without having the camphor tree's branches for support. Frowning with repulsion, he tried shaking the bloody bandage from his right hand, but to no avail. He finally ended up stooping down and scraping the bloody bandage off on the icy snow. *Where am I?* he thought, trying not to be alarmed but, rather, to attempt recognition by studying his surroundings more. Even in his nightmares, Marion tried to keep his wits about him.

As he couldn't make out where he was in the snow which had started falling more steadily within seconds while the snow beneath his feet seemed to grow murkier, Marion decided the only course of action was to move onward—-even though it meant giving up the camphor tree for balance should the need arise again. As Marion was no coward, he bravely trudged through the snow and ice to find out what his dream/nightmare wanted him to see— though the visibility was poor due to such heavy snowfall.

Before long, Marion was relieved to come to a clearing of some sort. And, as the snow wasn't falling as much at that point, he could actually see fairly clearly again. Walking into the clearing, the scenario suddenly started changing quickly around him. Where there'd been snow and ice, patches of green grass started to grow, and where there'd been only trees from the surrounding forest on the other side of the clearing, there was now a large body of water. Maybe a lake. Marion couldn't be sure yet. But most amazing of all, is that in the center of the clearing, a large stone monument (best Marion could make out) started piercing its way through the newly greened earth. It looked like an obelisk to Marion at first. Obelisk, he was surprised at another vocabulary word he'd naturally pulled out of his head, thanks to his teacher's recent vocabulary test in real life.

However, the obelisk didn't remain an obelisk for long. Instead, it suddenly fell on its side and started resembling a stone sarcophagus. *How strange*, Marion thought to himself. But what was even stranger was that he suddenly saw a man sitting on the stone coffin. Marion was sure he wasn't there before. *Hey, where did he come from?* Marion barely had time to think before the man startled him by speaking.

"Boy, come here," the young man beckoned, tilting his head back in the sunshine, as if to absorb more of the sun's rays, whilst remaining sitting atop the stone coffin. Though Marion thought the chap (yes, that was the word for lack of a better one that came to Marion's mind in describing the man dressed in old-fashioned clothing) seemed nice enough, he didn't exactly like the fact that the strange man was sitting on what looked to be an ancient stone coffin.

"Look here, mister, I know I'm probably dreaming this whole thing up, but I don't exactly care to approach strangers who happen to be sitting on stone coffins–that somehow morphed from obelisks–when I'm awake or when I'm asleep."

At that, the youthful-looking man jumped off of the sarcophagus with, "You've got a point there, lad." And, before dream-Marion could blink, the stranger was practically in front of him. He'd moved that fast. "You are my counterpart, boy," the man offered next.

"Your counterpart?" Marion questioned, racking his brain to see if there were an obscure meaning for counterpart that was eluding him. The only thing he knew counterpart to mean was two people sharing similar characteristics. And, he doubted he had much in common with the grown man before him. After all, Marion had just turned 12 years old, and he didn't exactly fancy sitting on stone coffins in the midst of strange forests.

As if he could read Marion's dream thoughts/process, because, indeed, he could, the young man bellowed with laughter, "That's rich young man. I don't always seek out stone coffins for chairs in the midst of strange forests. Me atop sarcophagi serves a purpose. But, I'm not here to talk about me. I'm here to talk about YOU!"

The man's voice had gotten so loud that Marion was sure he'd wake up soon from this strange dream/nightmare, but he didn't. Much as he wanted to at that point because although he wasn't fearful of the man, he felt like he was about to get schooled by him in some way. The stranger reminded Marion of teachers he'd had who'd goaded him into learning, so he wouldn't feel like an ignoramus. Not easily intimidated, however, Marion countered with," Look, I'll be happy to hear what you have to say—if you take it down a decibel or two."

"Fair enough," the man laughed. "Well, for starters, I guess, my name is Vasario."

"I'm Marion."

"I know."

"Clearly you have the advantage then because I have no idea who you are and why you've invaded my dream."

"Not so much of an invasion, Marion, as it is to help you and her."

"Me and who?"

"You and the young vampire girl. To be more precise: I am here to help you help her!"

"Seriously?! I don't know any young vampire girls—or old vampire women for that matter," Marion retorted, being a bit of a smart aleck due to being annoyed at the man's clearly, to him anyway, farfetched story.

"Ha!" Vasario answered, "I remember being impudent in my youth, too, but it didn't get me very far." At that comeback, Marion decided to shut up and listen more. "Ah, so now I have your attention. Good! You see those beautiful creatures over there?" Vasario pointed to the body of water which Marion had noticed earlier.

"I see the water," Marion responded. "But I don't see anything else."

"Then go closer, but not too close. Water vampires are quite beautiful, but they can also be quite deadly. Therein lies the rub."

"So, the young vampire girl you spoke of is a water vampire?"

"Great gods, no!" Vasario exclaimed. "But soon she'll come into contact with them, and you, my boy, will be the only one who'll be able to protect her."

"So, she's a different kind of vampire?"

"Yes, she's a Psychic Vampire."

"And, have I met her?"

"Yes."

"Where?"

"That doesn't matter right now. We haven't much time. I need to tell you about the water vamps, and how our kind function."

"Our kind?"

"Yes, you do realize that you're like me, right, Dear Boy?"

"Not really," Marion answered, trying to refrain from further verbal jabs. So, he switched gears and went along with what the strange man was saying with, "Okay, then, in what ways are we similar?"

"Now, that's a good question," Vasario answered, smiling broadly. "Well, for one, we are both shape-shifters. For another, we are both Therians—some call us Horusians. There are other names for us, too—though they aren't entirely accurate: Werewolves and Dogs, for instance."

"Are you saying I'm a werewolf?"

"Not exactly, Marion."

"You see, our kind can change into many things: wolves, dogs, cats, etcetera. We were most often recognized throughout history in our wolf form for some reason—probably because predatory wolves caused the most concern for the keepers of cattle. Calling us werewolves or dogs is really an incomplete assessment."

Marion was amazed that he could feel his relationship with Vasario growing less and less contentious by the minute. Plus, he couldn't believe he'd actually used another one of his vocabulary test words in a sentence: contentious! He smiled in his dream, and Vasario smiled back at him. "So, what do you want me to learn about the water vampires?"

As if right on cue, Marion and Vasario saw a large ebony creature. It kind of reminded Marion of the large sea serpents he'd seen in some of his fantasy books, except for this one looked like it had wings or strange fins, jump out of the water, hover in the air for a second with some kind of metal rod flashing in the sunshine with him and then plunge right back into the water. Then, looking directly at Marion to make sure he had his full dream-attention, Vasario said with mixed parts awe and warning, "That, my boy, is a water vampire!"

"So, I take it they don't like our kind, Therians, right?"

"Right. But, it's not like they've singled us out, exactly, either. They don't even like other kinds of vampires, for the most part."

"Like the vampire girl you mentioned. You mean they don't like her, even though she's a Psychic Vampire."

"That's basically right. You see, there are many different kinds of vampires. Some are benevolent and have learned how to use their gifts, and others are not."

"Are all Therians good?"

"No, not all, My Boy. But, we are...because we've chosen to be."

"I see. And, the vampire girl? She's chosen to be good...like us?"

"Yes."

"What's her name, and where did I meet her?"

"Patience, boy. I must tell you about the water vampires first. Did you see what the water vampire had attached to him?"

"I didn't even realize it was a him, but it did look like he was carrying a trident or something."

"Yes, that's their metal. It's attached to them around puberty."

"You mean their trident, I mean metal thingy, is actually attached to their arm?" Marion asked, not able to conceal the horror in his dream voice. "How and does it hurt?"

"Let me start at the beginning. You've heard of sirens, correct?"

"Of course, but I never thought they were real," Marion answered, careful not to come across as too flippant now. He had a growing respect for Vasario, so he'd decided to respond as politely as he could, under the somewhat dire dream circumstances.

"Well, they are. And, so are vampires, but I believe we've already established that."

"Yes."

"Well, once upon a time, a male vampire fell in love with the sweet song of a female siren. And, 18 months later they gave birth to the first water vampire."

"Was it a Psychic Vampire?"

"Good question," Vasario answered, beaming admiration towards his pupil and kin. "But, no. It was a vampire of purer bloodlines, with no purely human in the mix. But, as sirens are half raven and half human, the water vamps do resemble humans slightly. But, most of them got the predatory nature of both sirens and vampires. There are exceptions, however, and it really depends on how they're raised and the choices they make. Much as it is in any species."

"So, I saw the water vampire over there jump out of the water and into the sun's rays. I take it the sunlight isn't deadly to them, then?"

"Another good question!" Vasario exclaimed, with a bit of healthy pride heard in his voice for Marion. "And, the answer is: it depends on what kind of water vampire you're referencing. You see there are regular water vampires—about 75 % of their population is the regular kind, I think, though I'm not sure—and then there are the 'sol water vampires.'"

"Sol, as in sun?" Marion chimed in.

"Exactly, the sol water vampires are able to withstand the sun's rays, whereas the regular water vampires cannot."

"Why is that?"

"Because some, the sol water vampires, take more after their siren ancestors genetically (who could be out in the sun for hours, even days—they even loved sunning on rocks, in fact), but most take after their vampire ancestors (the purebred kind) genetically, and they cannot withstand the sunlight."

"Then, what about the Psychic Vampires—and the Psychic Vampire Girl, in particular, who you say I must protect...can she go out in the sunlight?"

"Yes because she's in large part human, not a purebred vampire, so her human blood allows her to be out in the sunlight. But, back to the water vampires...they don't have regular fangs, either."

"I'm not sure I even know what 'regular fangs' are, but I'll take your word for it."

"Yes because it won't be long before you wake up, and that's not as important as getting the crucial information delivered to you."

"I'm still listening," Marion said patiently.

"As the sirens were half raven and half woman, some of their birdlike traits got passed on to the water vampires. Instead of regular vampire fangs, water vampires have only three beak-like fangs which pierce through their upper gumline, and they have absolutely no teeth or fangs on their bottom gumline. This makes sinking their beak-like fangs into prey challenging–if it weren't for their metal."

"What I saw gleaming in the sunlight? The thing I thought was a trident?"

"Yes."

"And, what about the tail...it looked almost like a serpent's tail...or maybe a dragon's, as I thought I might have seen a barb on the end."

"Yes, purebred vampires could morph into dragons. The tail is from that, but that's not really vital information–there are more important things you must know."

"I'm guessing that metal that grows in their flesh, which reminds me of a trident...I'm guessing they use their metal to help steady their prey so that they can sink their three beak-like fangs into their unfortunate victim."

"Exactly...you're a quick study, Marion."

"Their metal finds them when the time is right. Water vampires are known for hoarding treasure in underwater caves. It must be the dragon connection, via their pureblood vampire ancestors, as dragons love hording treasure in caves above water," Vasario mused, before bringing himself back to his important task: namely, making sure Marion got all the pertinent information to enable him to be well-armed with knowledge when he encountered water vamps in the real world.

"What kind of metal finds them?" Marion was quick to ask, as he had been allergic to silver since he'd been a child.

"There are all kinds, but the metal must find them. Around puberty, the water vampires hear their ancestor's siren songs and are led to the proper metal for them. The metal is then thrust through the lower part of their palm and into the space between their radius and their ulna."

"Ouch! Do you mean that their trident thingy, I mean their metal, is thrust BETWEEN their two lower arm bones?"

"That's precisely what I mean."

"No wonder the water vampires aren't the happiest campers out there."

"Indeed, but it's a process that all water vampires readily embrace."

"Does the metal grow as they grow?"

"Yes, and the metal will grow larger and longer as the water vampire grows into adulthood, resembling grand tridents with three prongs oftentimes, or sometimes even more. They also take much pride in their prongs which many of them refer to as their tines. In fact, the more courageous the water vampire is, the larger, longer and more ornate his or her 'metal' is and the more tines they have. Plus, it doesn't take as long for it to grow."

"What about their wingy-fins? Like those I saw on the water vampire here?"

"They're not that important. But, what is is their 'metal'...you have realized by now, my dear boy, that our kind doesn't fare so well around silver, yes?"

"I've been allergic to it since childhood."

"Yes, me, too...most Therians are. It can even be deadly to Therians in large amounts. So steer clear of that kind of metal when you can."

"Believe me, I will."

"Another thing: our kind thrives on sunlight, so whenever you're in a battle situation, search for the sun's rays to give you strength."

"No wonder I'm such an outdoorsman," Marion volunteered.

"Right, me, too! But back to the water vampires. As you know, most water vampires, the regular water vampires, cannot tolerate the sunlight, but the sol water vampires can, so that makes them seem less destructible at first, but they are born with a weakness which the regular water vampires don't have: feathers at the nape of their necks. It's a throwback to their raven-siren blood. Plucking their feathers weakens them in various ways."

"Okay, got it, pluck the feathers at the napes of the necks of the sol water vamps, but what about the psychic vampire girl...who is she?" Marion questioned again, feeling that he'd been taught all that he needed to know about the water vampires and much more than he ever wanted to know.

"No time...must go...birthday..." was all that Vasario could convey before the dreamscape faded before Marion's eyes, and he was once again in his own bed, in his own bedroom, but strangely enough still wearing the boots from his dream, and they were covered in pluff mud encrusted with icy snow. Not caring to have his dad scold him for wearing dirty boots to bed, and really not wanting to explain that he didn't in reality, as he'd gone to bed like every other night in his pajamas and bare feet, he quickly went to his adjoining bathroom to clean off the grungy boots.

CHAPTER FOUR

South of Broad Birthday Party

Circumstances had changed quite a bit for Robyn and her family over the last year, ever since her 11th birthday party. Her mother, Leticia Lucas, had decided to list their house with Andrew Simons after all, due to her house value skyrocketing in the downtown area. She knew selling it would enable her and her children to never have to worry about finances again, and she could get a bigger house for them in West Ashley (about a half hour away from their old house in Downtown Charleston) along with lots more land. Two acres, to be exact. Lots of land to expand her organic garden, and she was even able to buy a greenhouse, for her precious Roman roses and lots of other kinds of roses (sadly, thorns for her were a prerequisite)—and, though she grew many kinds of vegetables for her family to eat, she didn't bother with growing other flowers, besides her precious roses. The great offer on their downtown house was one she truly couldn't, and didn't, refuse!

But their new house and land situation wasn't the only thing that had changed. Robyn's school situation had changed drastically, too. Robyn had decided to enroll at Porter Gaud and leave home-schooling behind. Leticia thought it a good idea as well. Home schooling had always been Robyn's choice, not Leticia's, so the transition made sense. Robyn felt that it was time she interacted more with kids her own age, so that's what she did. And, one of the kids her own age she happened to interact with quite a bit now was one Marion Simons.

Recently, Marion had handed out birthday invitations to everyone in his class for his 12th birthday party. Though he wasn't close to everyone, he thought it would be pretty rude not to invite all 44 students in his class. Private schools generally had much smaller classes than public schools, so if he'd gone to a public school then he might not have had that option. And, since Marion's birthday (October 27th) fell so close to Halloween (October 31st), he thought it might be fun to make it a Halloween-themed birthday party. As in, everyone would dress up in costumes and have birthday cake and then participate in both birthday and Halloween games, etcetera. Andrew Simons approved of his son's idea, so it was on in a major way, and many of the Porter Gaud kids in his class were excited about it.

Among those excited about going, was an overweight kid named Wil Lamely. His full name was Wilhelm Law Lamely, as he was named after one of his ancestors who'd been deceased for more than a few centuries. His mother found the peculiar name when researching her husband's genealogy–shortly before giving birth to her son, Wilhelm Law Lamely. Just because a kid didn't exactly fit in looks-wise was no reason to shun them in Robyn's mind, so she always tried to include Wil in activities at school. Many of both her and Marion's classmates deliberately avoided him, though. And, some had good reason, for he'd become a big bully to offset his low self-esteem.

As he kind of had a crush on Robyn, because she was pretty and nice to him, he made sure to ask her what she'd be wearing to the Halloween-themed birthday party at Marion's house for his 12th birthday. Robyn replied with, "I'm going as a ghost since we celebrate Samhain at my house. It's a celebration of the dead, simply put, and it's the time when spirits and faeries are said to be able to pass through a 'door' in their dimension to our world."

"What? You mean you celebrate Samhain rather than Halloween? Is Samhain even Christian?" Wil Lamely forcefully asked.

"Not that I owe you any explanation, but since I'm proud of my heritage and our faith, I'll just say that Samhain is NOT Christian." Robyn knew better than to stay and explain further, as she doubted that Wil's fundamentalist Christian upbringing would allow him to open his mind much if he were resistant, as it seemed he was by the forcefulness he'd asked the question.

As Robyn walked away, she could hear Wil muttering under his breath, "Well, Samhain sounds like a satan celebration to me." And, she was so happy she'd made the choice to leave him when she had, as she didn't have the time or patience for ignorance like that! She believed in being nice to those who reciprocated kindness. It was fine if they were outsiders, as she'd been for years being home-schooled, but they had to be respectful ones.

Robyn caught up with her friends, Molly and Candace, while switching out books for her next class at her locker. "Hey, Robyn, you excited about Marion's birthday bash?" a breathless, from being a bit overweight and having two classes close together on the opposite sides of the school, Molly managed to get out—behind her locker's door to the left of Robyn's locker.

"Well, yeah, now that I have my costume picked out. What are you going as?"

"I was thinking of going as a vampire," Molly said softly, waiting to see how her friend would react. "Do you think that it's too 'out-there' for Charleston—especially with it being a South of Broad Halloween-Birthday party?"

Robyn rolled her eyes and replied, "If you ask me, Charleston needs to get a little more 'out-there,' as in with the times...it's the '80s after all...I love it...your idea...yes, it's out there...a necessary 'out there'!"

"Here, here," Candace chimed in. "As if we're not 'out-there' enough being the only public lesbian couple our age here!" And with that Candace, moving from her locker to the right of Robyn's locker and bypassing Robyn, quickly gave Molly a kiss on her cheek. "You know, out of the closet, out here, out there...as long as it's out!" And, at that, all three of them burst into peals of laughter. When their laughter subsided, Candace said, feigning having had her feelings hurt, "Hey, you didn't ask me what I'm going as."

Playing along, Robyn smartly answered, "Maybe I didn't care to know!" And, at that all three burst into laughter again.

"Oh yeah?! Well, now you're gonna know, whether or not you want to," Candace said with a broad smile. "I'm going as a zombie."

"Great gods," Robyn teased, "that's even more 'out-there' than a vampire."

"What about you, Robyn" Molly asked, with her sweet Southern drawl.

"A ghost."

"Boring!" Candace teased, and that made the three of them fill the locker hall with laughter once again. After their laughter subsided again, Candace offered, "Hey, wonder what Marion will dress as for his own party?"

"Werewolf," Robyn blurted out, surprising herself that she'd answered so quickly.

"Oh, really...and, how do you know this 'insider' knowledge when the rest of us don't?" Molly teased softly, knowing well of the undeniable attraction between Robyn and Marion.

"I-I don't," Robyn stuttered, thinking to herself that she hoped she wouldn't start stuttering like her heinous Uncle Jonas. Heinous, not because he stuttered, but because he was hateful! "I just think that Marion would make a great werewolf...I don't know why...maybe because he reminds me of a big puppy dog?"

"Maybe because he has puppy dog eyes for YOU!" Candace teased with incredulous laughter.

Robyn blushed a little, and feeling her discomfort, Molly put her arm around her with, "Candy, please, not everyone is as 'out' about their feelings as you!"

Candace looked down and said, "Well, okay, I'll take it down a notch." Molly had a way of toning down her bravado to exactly the right degree.

"Thanks, baby," Molly said, giving Candace's hand a thankful squeeze. Looking at the two of them together, Robyn could only hope for a great relationship like theirs one day.

"Okay, girls, see you later...I'm late for class," Robyn admitted, as she closed her locker and went down the hallway to the left.

Robyn realized how much she missed Downtown Charleston on the way to Marion's birthday party, and, even though she'd lived in a section of 'Downtown Chucktown,' on Nassau Street, it wasn't nearly as swanky as his section of Downtown Charleston, on Murray Boulevard, with the grand, refurbished Southern houses. However, she used to visit Murray Boulevard regularly and frequently passed by Marion's beautiful Italian Renaissance house, which many just referred to as a downtown waterfront mansion, on the way to White Point Gardens; it was really White Point Garden (singular) but many Native Charlestonians referred to it as plural. It was there at White Point Garden where she, her mother and Baby Sean would have picnics every other month or so. She had no idea that the beautiful Italian Renaissance house was Marion's house till after her 11th birthday, when her mother had received Andrew Simon's business card with his address and telephone number on it.

Robyn loved picnicking at White Point Garden with all the green grass, old oak trees with Spanish moss and crushed oyster shells along the paths. Not to mention, she still loved playing on the numerous Civil War-era cannons with Baby Sean and pretending that she was a pirate like the infamous 'gentleman' pirate who was hung there in the early 18th century: Stede Bonnet. She had to admit that she admired some outlaws, like Stede Bonnet and Robin Hood, though she wasn't exactly sure why. Plus, she loved walking up the grey chipped-paint stairs to the open area of the gazebo-like bandstand to take in the wondrous view as she looked past either High Battery or Low Battery, depending on which direction she turned, to see Charleston Harbor, where the Ashley and Cooper Rivers empty into the Atlantic Ocean. So much water...she always wondered what went on beneath it...

Andrew Simons had spared no expense for his son's 12th Halloween-ish Birthday Bash! He had a huge birthday cake with brown werewolves–since he knew that his son loved them (in fact, enough to even dress up as one for his own costume birthday party!) and it was a Halloween-themed Birthday Party after all– made of edible modeling clay placed strategically atop the three-tiered cake covered in orange fondant...there was even green grass made of edible modeling clay sticking out in some sections. When Robyn saw it, her mouth was agape for a second before she exclaimed, "This is too awesome to actually eat...I hope you have another 'regular' cake for eating."

"Are you kidding...I'll take a piece right now!" she heard obnoxious Wil Lamely, who'd sidled up to her left side, say. "And, make sure to give me one of the werewolves to eat, too" the gluttonous boy demanded. Even though Lamely had rather stealthily advanced to her side, Robyn noticed with some disgust that there was nothing furtive in the way he inhaled the large piece of cake he'd been given.

Seeing her chance to escape Lamely's negative energy, Robyn was relieved to see her friends Molly and Candace at the front door of Marion's house. Waving to them joyfully, she left Wil Lamely's side and hurried to go greet them with hugs. "So good to see you girls!" Robyn exclaimed.

"What...did we rescue you from Lame Boy's clutches?" Candace boldly teased.

Molly gave Candace a playful jab in the belly to tone it down some, but Robyn just laughed and responded with, "More like I was afraid of what I'd do to HIM if y'all hadn't arrived."

"Touche!" Candace responded, with even more respect for Robyn.

"So, has Lamely left us any cake?" Molly asked softly with a smile.

"Don't know, but you two are more than welcome to head over there and see. Me? Well, I'm happy to have escaped...think I'll go and see how the birthday boy's doing," Robyn said, walking away with a smile and a spring in her step.

Marion was talking to a group of guys from school who were encircling him and looking at his birthday gifts. He'd taken off the head to his werewolf costume, and he was thinking of taking off the entire costume and just change into his jeans and a t-shirt because it was way too hot—a heavy costume like that—for subtropical Charleston, South Carolina weather—even in late October! Robyn seeing beads of sweat rolling down Marion's face couldn't resist commenting, "Hey, I didn't know werewolves sweat like humans."

"Yeah, well, I'm pretty sure even real werewolves would be sweating in Charleston humidity!" Marion countered, with a big grin, revealing his naturally long and pointed cuspids.

"You've got a point there, and so do most of the Charleston ghosts, I'm sure," Robyn said, seriously thinking about taking off her own ghost costume, too. Then changing her mind, as she looked over at Candace and Molly eating cake in their get-ups she offered, "Well, I suppose if a vampire and a zombie can tough out the Charleston heat, then we can, too."

"I guess you're right...I mean, we have central air and all, but it's still hot in here," Marion admitted. "Wonder if it would be totally wrong if I left my own party to trot down to High Battery to cool down with the breeze off of the water."

"Yeah, that would be so NOT right," Robyn said with a smile. "But it is tempting!"

"So," Marion said, looking at Robyn intensely, "when my party starts to wind down in a little while, would you like to take a walk with me along the Battery?"

"I don't know..." Robyn began, "I mean, doesn't that seem kinda Southern Belle-ish—taking a promenade down the seawall. I am most certainly NO Southern Belle." Robyn began toying with the sterling silver bracelet her mother had given her, as it was a nervous habit she'd developed. Her mother playfully teased that the bracelet was her security blanket. And, Robyn was a bit

uncomfortable with flirting, or with those flirting with her as was
the case, so her bracelet was certainly getting a workout–with it
being twisted around her wrist a lot at that point.

"I know THAT, and I really dig that you are NOT, it's
just...that, well, it's my birthday, you know...that could be my
birthday gift from you," Marion said slyly, with a wink. He felt it
was time to take their relationship further. He wanted to let her
know that he'd had a crush on her since HER birthday–when they
first met.

"But I already got you a gift," Robyn retorted, with a gleam in
her eye.

"I didn't realize that there's a 'birthday rule' where I can only
get one gift from the same person," Marion countered.

"Ha! You got me there...we'll walk later then, Wolf Boy...and
when we do...try to keep up, please" Robyn added, as she walked
away jauntily.

CHAPTER FIVE

Sol Water Vamps

Same Day
(October 27, 1986)
Different Place
(In the Water, Near White Point Garden)

Raven Blackfeathers had recently heard the call from his ancestors: the Sirens. They were technically Spirit Sirens, as they were no longer in physical form and were perhaps at least a millennia or two old. He'd been summoned to one of the water vampire treasure caves beneath the water, and it was there that he found the perfect 'metal' rod 'singing' to him. It didn't actually sing, but that's what the water vamps referred to it as. In actuality, it vibrated back and forth and made a sound almost like chimes would in the process of its agitation against the wall of the underground cave. This was a special kind of metal; it was sentient metal.

Raven remembered asking his teacher after class one day, about a year before his own metal 'sang' to him, if water vampires' special metal was anthropomorphic, since they'd recently had anthropomorphic as a word to define on a vocabulary test at Fort Moultrie Preparatory School for Water Vampires. His teacher said it was a good question but that water vampires' unique metal rods were not anthropomorphic because they probably existed long before water vampires came into existence, and rather than the metal having 'water vampire attributes,' perhaps water vampires had special metal attributes which accounted for their symbiotic relationship. Raven remembered thinking that it was certainly something to consider, and he marveled at how much he really didn't know about the world after all. For instance, he lived underwater, and he had heard tales all his life of the different kind of worlds above the waves—namely, in the air and on dry land. He couldn't imagine it being much of a life, with no oyster shell beds to sleep on with soft seaweed for mattresses and blankets, etc. but he was curious about all life and that included the life-forms on dry land, too.

When he came upon his own 'singing metal' rod, he knew what to do. It was perhaps the most painful part of puberty, and puberty for water vampires was a little earlier than for humans, as he'd recently turned just 12 years old, that any water vampire would experience. The insertion of one's metal into one's arm. Water vampire arms were much like human arms, in that they had many of the same bones. With his physiology being similar to a human's, in the top half of his body, at any rate, it's not surprising that Raven Blackfeathers also had a palm, a radius and an ulna. Yet, unlike a human, when the metal that found him, by its singing, was thrust into his palm and between his radius and ulna, it was made to be inserted there, as it started to wrap around his bones like roots and actually grew out more through his wrist, almost as tree branches would, as he grew and through Raven's acts of bravery. It was a perceptive metal that reacted by growing longer and more ornate the more courageous its water vampire was; it was a symbiotic relationship, to be sure. And the water vampire historic records were unclear as to how the relationship had begun. But this much is sure: water vampires were dependent on their metal if they were to become hunters of any real worth in their underwater society.

Raven was still primarily feeding off of smaller underwater creatures, like most water vampires his age, like fish, jellyfish and crabs. But, he longed for the day when his metal would grow into a multi-tined weapon. When that happened, he'd more easily be able to feed off of dolphins, sharks, etcetera. Carrying a trident wasn't the same as having a sentient metal which grew to resemble a trident in looks there to help water vampires really anchor their prey and also to sense, at times, prey, even before it moved, for the water vampires to track...the metal would sometimes vibrate between the radius and ulna bones of their chosen water vampire to let their water vampire know that a meal was nearby.

Even though Raven hadn't been united with his metal for long, it had already alerted him to nearby appropriate prey with its vibrations. In fact, he'd been one of the youngest water vampires to ever successfully catch and drain the blood from a large octopus.

This was unusual because of the octopus' large size and the fact that octopi are known for their intelligence and ability to outmaneuver many foes—like water vamps and humans. Though Raven knew of water vampires who didn't drain their prey completely, to let them live, it unfortunately wasn't a common practice. And, he most certainly wasn't the compassionate kind of 'above-water' vampire like Setiana had chosen to be. Many in the water vampire community still erroneously saw compassion as weakness—even though oftentimes their 'metal' tried to show them otherwise.

It wasn't just Raven's hunting abilities that set him apart from many of the other water vampires. It was also the fact that he was one of the rare sol water vampire variety. He'd long been able to hunt fish close to the surface, as he never had to worry about being burned by the sun's rays should he accidentally jump up and out of the water during the daylight hours. Unlike the regular water vampires who ended up smelling a lot like grilled fish if they ever pierced through the surface of the water during the daylight hours. Sunset was a different story, as sol water vamps and regular water vamps enjoyed jumping out of the water and diving back in in the moonlight—oftentimes until dawn. Many regular water vampires slept in the day and hunted at night, as mostly nocturnal creatures, because of this, but sol water vampires could basically choose what time for sleep suited them the best. Diffused sunlight, however, much like the reflected sunlight of the moon, through the water didn't bother even the regular water vamps—though their eyes tended to be more photosensitive than the more rare sol water vampires since they were primarily nocturnal. It was just the direct rays, if the regular water vampires happened to be on the water's surface or above the surface, that did more than scorch them. Direct sunlight burned regular water vampires, whereas it did not the fortunate sol water vampires.

Before a water vampire got their metal, they would generally catch their prey with their bare hands and then rather awkwardly bite into it with their three beak-like fangs on their upper gumline. Regardless of whether a water vampire was a regular water vampire or a sol water vampire, they all were born with just the three strange beak-like fangs, as a genetic atavism to their siren blood. They had no other teeth, fangs or otherwise. It made their catching and eating (technically by drinking), by draining the blood of their prey, challenging—at least until they got their sentient metal. As they generally just drained their prey of blood, they didn't have to worry about chewing what they'd managed to catch and hold. Yet, using underwater spears and such, before getting their attached 'metal,' was a much more awkward way to hunt, and it wasn't nearly as successful since the spears and such they fashioned were not sentient–like their unique 'metal.'

Most water vampires, regular or sol, were born with scaly black skin–in various shades of black. As their ancestors were Sirens (half Raven and half Human), it made sense. Raven Blackfeathers' skin was a beautiful dark, almost blue-black at times, hue beneath the water, and when he surfaced in the sunlight, his platelike dermal structures frequently shimmered iridescently.

The only real downside to being born a sol water vampire versus a regular water vampire was the fact that sol water vamps also had three black feathers at the nape of their neck–also a genetic atavism (another vocabulary word that Raven's teacher had given on a test in his Fort Moultrie Preparatory School for Water Vampires–named after the Fort the humans had built above their underwater classrooms) from their Siren bloodlines.

While many considered the three feathers attractive to look at, it was the more sinister, at least from a water vampire's point of view, attributes they were capable of which concerned many sol water vamps. Legend had it, as no sol water vampire that Raven ever knew of personally had ever experienced it, that whomever plucked the feathers from the nape of a sol water vampire's neck was endowed with some of the aspects of a sol water vampire. One of them being the ability to swim above water in the sunlight, depending on which feather was plucked, so it had become a law long ago that no regular water vampires were to pluck a sol water vampire's feathers just to have that *temporary* power. In fact, it was an offense punishable by death, so Raven knew of no regular water vamp in recent history who'd even attempted it. But the real threat, through the horror stories Raven had grown up hearing, was not from the regular water vampires, but from the humans and some above water/ground vampires who could harness the various powers of the sol water vampires if they plucked their feathers, too. And, it wasn't all the horror stories he'd heard of humans and even other species of vampires (who weren't water vampires). Having one's feathers plucked as a sol water vampire was not only painful, but it was considered a disgrace and unsightly. Besides those facts, it also greatly weakened the sol water vampire, whose feathers had been plucked, by at least temporarily taking away some of their natural attributes. The feathers were each said to contain different magical properties–so they could greatly benefit those who did the plucking and holding on to them. What those magical properties were, Raven didn't know, and he never wanted to find out either! Even talk of plucking the feathers of a sol water vampire was, in many ways, a taboo subject in the water vampire community at large.

Raven's reverie was interrupted by something he saw gleaming about 100 yards away–on the sand embankment–below where the humans had built part of their Low Battery Walkway. He was warned to never get too close to the railings of Low Battery or High Battery, as there were many rocks, and it was wise to never get too close to the human creatures he'd also been warned. But his love for treasure won over the cautionary council from the elder water vampires, so he swam under water until he had to come out of it to rest on the sand to gauge exactly what kind of treasure he was looking at–its silver surface gleaming in the sunlight delighted him. He'd never seen treasure like this in any of the water vampire caves he'd visited, and he'd seen plenty of treasure in the form of gold coins, silver coins, gold blocks, silver blocks, pearls by the pound, etcetera. Seeing strange looking creatures walking on two legs in the distance, who he assumed were humans from descriptions in legends and the history he'd studied in his Fort Moultrie Prep. School for Water Vampires, but fast approaching the section of the Low Battery Promenade above him, he realized he had to get the treasure and go before they saw him. He doubted any of his water vamp friends had ever been that close to the creatures, and he hoped his metal would grow because of what he considered his bravery in getting the strange treasure, but it didn't. His metal was wise and considered Raven risking his safety, their safety, for a camera, for that is what the strange treasure was, extremely foolhardy. So, the metal didn't even grow a hair, much to Raven's dismay, but seeing the strap attached to the new shiny 'treasure' Raven looped it over his metal till it slid down to his wrist, and he quickly headed back into deeper water to show it to his friends.

CHAPTER SIX

Beneath the Water

Sirenetta Downing and Eric Plumago couldn't wait to follow their mutual sol water vampire friend, Raven Blackfeathers, to where he'd found his new treasure earlier that same day! It was valuable to them because it was different than anything they'd come across before, and it was so shiny! Water vampires loved all things shiny–probably because of their love of treasure—no matter that the old camera Raven had found was probably worth no more than $75.00 when it was brand new, as in, when the unfortunate tourist who had bought it the week before to take pictures on the Battery actually purchased it. The poor fellow had accidently dropped it in the water when he'd seen something he couldn't explain. He could swear he'd seen a mermaid or something with a trident in the distance, and he wanted to take a picture of it so that his friends and family wouldn't think him completely crazy! In his shock at what his eyes didn't want to believe, as he'd actually laid eyes on a sol water vampire in the distance, he'd dropped his camera over the rails to the right of the seawall promenade, also known as the Battery. It was definitely too treacherous to even consider going over the rails and dropping down to the sandbar and rocks below. Not to mention, the tourist didn't want to have a run-in with what he thought he saw in the waves.

Sirenetta and Eric both knew that their parents would not approve of getting that close to the human's walkway–even for new treasure–so they didn't want to wake their parents up to tell them where they were going. Raven had an insidious way of talking his closest friends, Sirenetta and Eric (who were also sol water vampires), into just about anything, and he assured them that he was not going to wake up his parents to tell them either. They admired what they took to be his bravery, so they followed him willingly. He didn't bother telling them that his metal had not grown at all after picking up the shiny new metal (the camera) earlier in the day, so it was really more reckless than anything else (and Raven knew it)–what they were attempting: going so close to humans in the hopes of finding more strange *treasure*.

It was a real problem for the adult regular water vampires who had sol water vampire offspring, as the adult regular water vampires generally slept during the day, safely away from the sun's rays, so they couldn't always keep up with everything their offspring were up to. Sirenetta and Eric's parents faced the same problem Raven's parents did; as regular water vampires they weren't generally around to monitor their sol water vampire progeny during the daylight hours. And, the problem was even more pronounced in the water vampire colonies where there were no adult sol water vampires, as was the case for the Charleston Water Vampire Territory. The closest adult sol water vampire lived beneath the waters near Beaufort, South Carolina, so he wasn't able to monitor the activities of the young sol water vampires living beneath the waters surrounding Charleston, South Caolina, as he belonged to the Beaufort Water Vampire Territory. The young sol water vampires, living in the waters surrounding Charleston, South Carolina on three sides (as it is a peninsula), of which there were only three (Raven, Sirenetta and Eric), were basically free to do as they chose during the daylight hours, despite the warnings from their caring parents.

"Look," Sirenetta gestured to both Raven and Eric, with her arm recently fused with her own 'magical metal,' "I think I see something gleaming over there." Eric and Raven saw it, too, and it was only slightly down (about 3 yards east) from where Raven had found his 'treasure' earlier that very day below the human seawall promenade, known as Low Battery.

Robyn couldn't believe her sterling silver bracelet was lost over the bars at Low Battery. *At least it wasn't over High Battery,* she fleetingly thought, as there was hardly any sandbar to fall on over there...just water, for the most part. And, the way it happened made both her and Marion turn red with the embarrassment of it! Marion had finally convinced Robyn to make good on the 'birthday walk (gift)' she'd promised him, and they managed to slip out of his house with nobody except Wil Lamely noticing–unbeknownst to either of them. As Lamely hadn't followed them right away,

Marion and Robyn thought they'd managed to escape unnoticed, so they'd started holding hands on the seawall promenade, staring out at the sparkling blue water together blissfully. What Robyn hadn't realized was that other things had been leading up to the fateful event of her losing her bracelet. A couple of things contributing were that in both playing incessantly with her bracelet as a nervous habit and having it get caught and loosened up further (the clasp) on her ghost outfit—as she took it off hastily to go and walk with Marion—were also factors in her losing her silver bracelet. She was merely thinking along the lines of being super happy to have the ghost costume off and that she was really happy she'd worn shorts and a t-shirt underneath. Likewise, Marion was more than happy to take off his hot werewolf outfit to just wear his shorts and t-shirt that he had on underneath.

"Looks like diamonds on top of the water today," Marion had offered, happy that Robyn had let him hold her hand.

"Yes, the sunlight's dazzling!" Robyn exclaimed. And, they both laughed for no real reason, except that they were truly happy to be alone together. When they got to the stairs leading from Low Battery to High Battery, Marion saw his opportunity to lean in for a kiss, as Robyn had stopped to lean back against the rails of Low Battery, to take in both Marion, at close range, and her favorite park, White Point Gardens, in the background. But, when Marion leaned in towards Robyn for a kiss, his hands also grasped hers and his arms pressed up against her arms, including the one with the sterling silver bracelet.

"Shitake mushrooms!" he exclaimed in pain, though he'd very much enjoyed their first kiss, as her bracelet left an angry red welt on his arm almost immediately.

And, then Marion remembered what that dream fellow, Vasario, had said, "...our kind doesn't fare so well around silver...."

While Marion was remembering Vasario's words, Robyn turned from him towards the water, embarrassed that their first kiss had turned out to be such an awkward one. She didn't understand what had caused him to scream out, "Shitake mushrooms!" But it didn't sound like anything good. She wondered if she'd accidentally bit his lip or something, but she didn't think that kind of thing would exactly be 'accidental' and she certainly didn't do anything like that on purpose. Worried, she twisted the real culprit, unbeknownst to her, her bracelet, as she gazed out at the water, unable to look at Marion due to her face being flushed from both the kiss and embarrassment. The silver clasp to the bracelet had had enough of the constant tugging, etcetera and released itself causing the bracelet to slip over Robyn's wrist, her hand and her fingers and onto the sandbar below. She watched in horror as the waves had already started lapping at the shiny gift from her mother.

"My bracelet," she said in horror, leaning dangerously over the rails, as if she intended to go and get it herself.

Alarmed, Marion offered, "If it means that much to you, then I could try and retrieve it for you." Then, realizing the danger to himself in more ways than one: actually getting down to the sandbar, avoiding rocks, before what looked to be high tide rolled in, and the fact that he'd just figured out that her bracelet was most likely silver. "It's silver, right?" he questioned, shaking his head.

"Why, yes, but that doesn't matter to me," Robyn answered, mistakenly thinking that Marion thought she wanted her sterling silver bracelet back because it was valuable monetarily. "It was a gift from my mother to me, but I suppose it holds so much value to me because *he* gave it to her."

"Who's..." Marion started to ask.

But before he even finished, Robyn interrupted softly with, "My father." Knowing how precious anything was from his own deceased mother, that was the catalyst that absolutely convinced Marion to jump over the rails next and down to the sandbar–about 12 feet below–before Robyn could even protest. Marion didn't care if the silver burned his hand or not, he was going to get Robyn her bracelet back–after knowing its history.

The good news was: Marion landed easily on the sand, with his feet sinking into it and his hands steadying himself, as he leaned slightly forward. Momentarily on 'all fours' Robyn was taken with his animal-like agility. The bad news was: as Marion reached out a hand to grasp the silver bracelet, he realized that he wasn't alone down where the sand and rocks met the water. Right before Marion was able to retrieve the silver bracelet, something resembling a metal-pronged rod speared it and dragged it into the water, but that wasn't the strangest thing: Marion saw what the metal rod was attached to: a female about his age, but she had gills, and a tail kind of like he'd seen on dragons in his fantasy books. The next second he realized that he was looking at what his Dream Guide, Vasario, had warned him about: a water vampire.

Funny, he'd never considered there would be female water vampires, too. But there Sirenetta was, almost as surprised as he was, for she'd heard that humans never went on the sandbanks below Low Battery, or High Battery for that matter.

Things might have remained about the same as they'd always been, if an unwisely bold notion hadn't crossed Sirenetta's mind: what if she drained an actual *human?!* Surely that would make her metal grow more quickly and ornately...more than that of any of the other water vampires' metal her age and even older! She didn't give much of a thought to the fact that she was being overly ambitious and foolhardy! *Such is the way of youth, even in water vampire culture at times,* her wise mother and father may have realized and said, but to no avail, as they were fast asleep underwater for the day on their big bed of oyster shells with seaweed wrapped tightly around them both for warmth.

Robyn had seen her bracelet looped around some metal, and was trying to grasp exactly what was happening when next she saw what looked almost like a girl her own age, but with long black hair that had seaweed and shells wrapped in it decoratively, grab Marion by the front of his shirt and pull him into the water with her! Robyn couldn't believe her eyes at first, but she didn't waste any time in moving so fast that Wil Lamely, who'd been following both her and Marion down the seawall sidewalk to spy on their activities, as he still had a crush on Robyn, only saw a blur as she jumped from the rails to the sandbar and into the water. She wasn't going to let anything happen to Marion on her watch. And, she had a feeling that Marion's very life depended on her help!

Somehow, Robyn's eyes adjusted fairly easily to being underwater. It wasn't like she had an extra clear lid like all water vampires were born with, but she somehow managed to see the female creature clearly—even underwater. She looked like an underwater dragon to Robyn, with her fins resembling wings almost, even though they clearly functioned as fins, too. If the creature weren't dragging her boyfriend deeper underwater to a possible death, then Robyn would have marveled at the creature's beauty and strength. And, as if one dragon-like underwater creature weren't enough to deal with, Robyn realized in horror that the female was swimming underwater, towards two male creatures who looked a lot like her, with a somewhat dazed Marion in tow. Marion hadn't been able to react as quickly as Robyn had,

with her super speed, but now that what was going on had really
sunken in, he decided to take action, as he felt fairly sure he was
dealing with the sol kind of water vampire because she'd been able
to withstand the sunlight with no problem when she grabbed him.
He heard Vasario's words repeated in his mind, "...they are born
with a weakness which the regular water vampires don't have:
feathers at the nape of their necks...Plucking their feathers
weakens them in various ways." Not wasting one more second,
Marion maneuvered himself closer to Sirenetta, by kicking his legs
under water, almost like dog paddling but without using his arms,
to her surprise, as prey didn't usually want to swim closer to their
captor.

Before Sirenetta fully realized what was happening, Marion
had drawn her body next to his, almost in an embrace, but instead
of kissing her, as he had Robyn, he quickly moved the hair floating
down her back to expose the nape of her neck. As he couldn't see
what he was doing, he only felt his way since she was facing him
underwater. He quickly felt for feathers at the nape of her neck.
He had to hurry, as he didn't know how much longer he could hold
his breath. He figured that a water vampire, like herself, might be
into draining his blood, but he had a more pressing concern.
Namely, he didn't want to drown first! He felt something at the
nape of her neck, and he wasn't even sure what he was feeling at
first because the feathers he'd felt had never been attached to
anything, and they'd been *dry* feathers. But the feathers he was
feeling were slick, almost like they'd been dipped in oil. Yet, he
didn't have time to marvel at what he was feeling. Marion knew he
had to take action quickly, so he grabbed onto all three feathers at
the nape of her neck and pulled with all his might. One slipped
through his hand and in doing so, he got a nasty cut. Like a paper
cut times 100! He could see his hand begin trailing blood in the
water as he tried to position himself to get a better look at it, as
Sirenetta had let go of him after her feathers were plucked–from
the pain and shock of having had that happen to her!

Besides the physical pain from having had two of her feathers
plucked, Sirenetta was in pure agony considering that she might
now become just a regular water vampire, but as she surfaced to
see if her ability to remain in the sunlight with no harm was still
intact, she was relieved to see that it was. She wasn't sure what it
meant to not have her other two feathers, besides the fact that it
was a literal pain in her neck, but she sighed with relief that she

still had her most important trait as a sol water vampire. And, in her relief, she wasn't even considering the powers that her former prey had now gained with her two feathers firmly grasped in his bleeding hand.

Whether Sirenetta's feathers were 'magical feathers' or just super scientifically advanced is uncertain, but their effects on Marion were undeniable. Within moments, he no longer felt like his lungs were going to explode; in fact, he found himself 'breathing' quite freely underwater. No need for him to even come up to the surface for air, as he had remarkably grown what could be considered large gills, for lack of the proper water vampire term, on either side of his neck. He figured that his transformation must be because of the feathers, or at least one feather, so he grasped them even more tightly in his hand. If one feather imbued him with the ability to breathe underwater, then he couldn't help wonder what 'magical' property the other feather would give him.

CHAPTER SEVEN

Castle Pinckney

Robyn was more than a little concerned seeing the trail of blood that Marion was leaving in the water ahead of her. She knew that amongst other worries, like the three seemingly brutal, underwater-dragon-like-mermaid creatures she'd spied, there were also sharks in the area. Retrieving her silver bracelet was at the bottom of her to-do list at that point; saving Marion being at the top! As she closed the gap between Marion and herself, she noticed that his former captor suddenly started swimming *away* from him.

She saw the female sea creature join two males about her same age, by the looks of things, about 100 yards from what she called Castle Pinckney–it was really Shutes' Folly Island (also known as Shutes Folly Island, she'd learned in school)–and they certainly looked like they were the same water species. Whatever they were! Robyn was almost beside Marion before she noticed the change in his appearance. "You've got...got gills," she managed to sputter out, along with some of the water she'd swallowed in her haste to rescue him. "But how? Pretty sure you never had those before."

It was easy for Marion to now breathe both below and above water, so he just remained there at the surface treading water while he explained. "I know this is gonna sound crazy, but that girl...that creature...and her two companions she's with now...over there," he said, gesturing to where Sirenetta had gone to catch up with her friends, Raven and Eric.

"Yes," Robyn interrupted, "looks like they've assembled near the small island I call Castle Pinckney...and...what the heck are those creatures?" Robyn asked, more than a little perplexed.

"Okay, this is gonna sound crazy, but..." Marion began.

"More crazy than brutal underwater dragon-like creatures?!" Robyn offered. "I doubt it can be crazier than what I've just seen.

Whatever they are, whomever they are, I've seen them...can still see them..."

"They're called water vampires."

"Well, that kinda makes sense," Robyn started, "but how the heck do you know that?"

"If we weren't in the midst of a possible life and death situation, then I might think it funny that you've said 'heck' two times in the last few minutes," Marion teased. "Okay, here's where it gets all crazy-sauce again: I learned about water vampires from a dream I had...there was this guy, Vasario, who warned me about them."

"That is weird, but not as crazy-sauce as you might think," Robyn consoled, thinking of her own strange dream with Setiana.

"Thing is, I was told to pull the feathers at the nape of their neck—in the dream—so that's what I did...I think it may have saved my life. Sorry about your bracelet, though...I think that female water vamp still has it."

"Oh, don't worry about that...I'm just glad you're okay," Robyn offered. "Did she hurt you? Your hand is bleeding."

"I cut my hand on one of her feathers...they're not like normal feathers. They're tough...like those creatures."

"But how did you grow gills?"

"That's it...the feathers have magical properties...I guess one of them gave me gills."

"That is crazy-sauce, but kinda cool," Robyn offered. "Wonder how long you're gonna have them?"

"Hopefully for as long as I need them out here in the water," Marion retorted. "I'll make sure to hold onto them tightly...who knows...maybe dropping them makes their power go away. There were three feathers, but I only plucked two."

"That's interesting...what does the second feather do if the first one gave you gills?"

"I'm not sure...maybe nothing to me, but she, the female water vampire, looked like she was in pretty bad shape after I plucked her two feathers. My dream guide guy, Vasario, told me that plucking their feathers weakens them or something like that."

"I guess that makes sense," Robyn replied. Then she added, "Well, about as much as any of this makes sense."

"What should we do about those three water vampires?" Marion asked next. "I mean, won't they be a threat to any human out in the surrounding Charleston waters?"

"I guess, but wouldn't they have been before today, too? I mean, why haven't we ever seen one before? And, why haven't any of their dead bodies ever washed up on shore?"

"I don't know," Marion said, after brief consideration, but then he remembered something he'd heard from some of those who consider Bigfoot to be real, too, "but maybe they bury their dead, so we aren't seeing the water vampire corpses."

"Or maybe they're like the other kind of vampires," Robyn thought, thinking of Setiana, "and live, or exist, for practically ever!"

"Are you sure you're gonna be okay without your bracelet...I mean, I could try and battle three water vampires—you say the word," Marion offered bravely.

"Don't be silly, a bracelet's a bracelet. You mean much more to me than that," Robyn admitted. Then to bring some much needed levity to the situation, she said with a twinkle in her eye, "Hey, let me see the gills you're sportin'. Can I touch 'em?" She asked next, treading water right in front of him.

"Yes, but it'll cost you a kiss."

"Just one?" Robyn countered. "You've got two gills, so shouldn't it be a kiss for each 'gill touch'?"

"You got me there," Marion smiled and then leaned in for his first of two kisses. It was a long kiss, too...at least 20 seconds or so. So long that they didn't notice the new company that Marion's bleeding hand was attracting. But they couldn't help but notice when both Marion and Robyn felt something brush by their legs. Both of their eyes had been closed for the kiss, but they both opened them and looked down at the water to see what had brushed by them. Their eyes opened in horror at what they saw: a shark! A shark had just brushed past them while they were kissing. "Good as that kiss was, we're gonna have to put the second kiss on hold."

"No kiddin'!" Robyn exclaimed. "But let's not panic just yet, as that was just a Bonnethead Shark. I mean, yeah it's a shark, but they're generally not aggressive towards humans."

"Well, that's a relief, at least," Marion admitted.

"Yeah, but we should really be heading back...there are others which aren't known to be as friendly to humans...especially bleeding humans," Robyn shared, looking at Marion's wounded hand.

"You mean like those?" Marion asked, pointing at the two new sharks which were headed their way and now blocking them from heading back to the Battery.

"Great Goddess!" Robyn exclaimed. "Now we do have to worry...those are Bull Sharks!"

"But, we have to go back that way to get back to the Battery."

"If we go back that way right now, then we may well be heading to Davy Jones' Locker instead," Robyn countered, grimly.

"But the only other way is towards them!" Marion exclaimed, pointing at the three young water vampires who still hadn't dispersed, but, rather, were waiting and watching them in front of the small island of Castle Pinckney.

"Well, you've successfully battled a water vampire before and come out on top," Robyn said, "so it seems like the best option—considering."

"Yeah, well, I battled just one, and it was kinda touch 'n' go there for some time, and now there are three of them!"

"Yeah, but you've got me this time, and we are armed with a certain amount of knowledge about them—I mean, with the feathers thing."

"I guess," Marion said with a great amount of trepidation still, "but that knowledge was imparted to me in a *dream!*"

"Well, it's seemed like pretty accurate information so far," Robyn said, thinking of her own dream meeting. "Who's to say it's any less valuable that what we've learned in school? You learned about water vampires in your dream, and I learned about shark identification in school. However we received the knowledge, they've both come in handy."

"Yeah, handy!" Marion laughed, while waving his bloody hand in the air...laughing made him relax enough to capitulate to Robyn's suggestion, so they made their way towards the three water vampires and Castle Pinckney.

Sirenetta's swimming abilities were almost nonexistent by the time she'd caught up with her water vamp pals, Eric and Raven. Alarmed, they'd helped her make it to the rocky shores, by each looping one of her arms over their shoulders and swimming her there, of Shutes Folly Island (which some referred to as simply Castle Pinckney), where Castle Pinckney, the small old masonry fortification was now being reclaimed by Mother Nature. On the way, she motioned for them to rise to the surface, as she was finding it hard to breathe under water then, too. She needed to breathe at the surface, as her gills were malfunctioning. The island was about 1.3 miles from the shoreline beneath the seawall promenade where Sirenetta had originally grabbed Marion.

"What–what did that thing..." began Raven, feeling an overwhelming concern for Sirenetta since he'd been crushing on her for years now.

"They're called humans, idiot!" Eric interrupted, as he, too, had been crushing on Sirenetta for years and didn't like that she and Raven had grown so close.

"Vamps, please!" Sirenetta exclaimed. "He got two of my feathers, that's why I'm not able to swim and breathe underwater now, I believe."

"What about your third?" Eric asked, with genuine concern.

"Still intact, thankfully, or I'm guessing I'd no longer be able to withstand the sun's rays with you here on this *rock*," Sirenetta said somewhat sarcastically in reference to the small island.

"So that human has your abilities now, at least two of them, right?" Raven asked, thoughtfully.

"Maybe, I guess...looks like he's been doing okay out in the water," Sirenetta retorted, rather absentmindedly, weakened from losing her natural abilities as a sol water vampire.

"What made you want to do something so dangerous, Sirenetta?" Eric asked, already knowing the answer.

"To make my metal grow, of course!" Sirenetta snapped, and then softened with, "Sorry, I guess I was overly ambitious."

"Yes!" Raven exclaimed, "But also very brave," he admitted, remembering his own quest for the new shiny metal (camera) on the shore below the Battery.

"Didn't help, though, because even after all that my metal didn't even grow one hair in length–not to mention NO new ornate design," she added.

"Our metals most certainly have minds of their own," Eric admitted. "And what they take for bravery, etcetera, doesn't always fit our expectations of the same." And, at that, all three of the ambitious sol water vampires let out a sigh.

"So what now?" Raven asked. "If the human drops your feathers, then you may get your full abilities back...seems like I heard that somewhere, sometime..."

"I certainly hope so, as I'm not much use to anyone, including myself, in this state," Sirenetta admitted.

CHAPTER EIGHT
The Second Feather

Sirenetta was realizing what a big mistake she made in foolishly thinking she could take on the human male to help grow her metal, as she was now considerably weakened physically (she was still resting on the rocks of Shutes' Folly Island while her friends worried about what they were all going to tell their parents, as losing feathers had never happened to any sol water vampires in their lifetime). Adding insult to injury, Sirenetta's metal was practically immobile in its disapproval. Generally all water vampires could feel the presence of their metal at all times, but Sirenetta couldn't even feel hers in her arm now. Obviously, it hadn't considered attacking the human a courageous undertaking. So, Sirenetta felt defeated both physically and mentally.

Just when Sirenetta thought things couldn't have got much worse, unless she'd lost her third feather, too, she saw that the two humans were making their way, not back to the seawall (the Battery), but towards Shutes' Folly Island, where she and her friends, Eric and Raven, were resting. Her first thought was that they were coming to finish her off, by plucking her third feather, but her second was more likely, in that it was they were coming to the island for refuge, as she could see then that they were being pursued by Bull Sharks and they were looking for a safe haven on the island, maybe within the ruins of Castle Pinckney. And, Sirenetta didn't feel quite as weak when she realized that she'd probably injured the human male, too, as he was leaving a trail of blood in his wake that was practically a dinner bell for the sharks.

"Great gods!" Raven exclaimed. "I can't believe they're headed this way."

"Yeah, but they may not make it. Those sharks are closing in on them," Eric offered. "And, what do they have to look forward to if they do make it to this island? I mean, we'll be waiting for them, right?" he asked, looking at Raven to make sure he was up to the task of attacking them, as clearly Sirenetta was in no position to.

"At the rate they're going there's no way they'll make it here...they're going too slow...the sharks'll get them," Raven said, feeling that the threat of the human presence had been averted. Meanwhile, he intended to see if he and his metal could spear a fish around the shoals of the island for Sirenetta to eat. He was hoping that some fresh blood might help revive her somewhat.

The hungry bull sharks were closing in on Marion and Robyn, and Robyn knew they wouldn't make it to Castle Pinckney (Shutes' Folly Island) at the rate they were swimming. All the sudden, she felt her Psychic Vampire power of super speed kick in, and she knew that if she were swimming alone, then she could easily outdistance the predatory sharks. But, there was no way she'd leave Marion out in the Charleston Harbor alone–as a shark's meal! So, she was bound and determined to swim with him–maybe him holding onto her shoulders as she swam? She thought it was worth suggesting, anyhow. And, there wasn't much time to explain her 'gift'–well, one of them at any rate. "Marion, I have this ability," she began.

"Yeah, I know," he said with a big grin, "you can move really fast."

"Right, so I didn't know that you knew about it," she admitted, looking at him strangely, as if she wondered what else he knew about her that she generally kept hidden. "Okay, that's strange that you knew, but no time to explain more...I've got to get you and your shark bait-hand outta here...pronto!"

"Yes ma'am...just tell me what to do," he said, loving the fact that Robyn was so able to take control of the dire situation.

"Hold onto my shoulders with your legs to the side, so that I can kick between them, and let me see if I can get us safely to Castle Pinckney at least." Marion did as Robyn suggested, and they were certainly making faster progress than before, but it wasn't fast enough. Robyn simply couldn't move as quickly towing Marion. And, as the bull sharks were just a few yards from them, they thought for sure that their young lives were over, but then something amazing happened. As Marion went to kick at one of the bull sharks, he realized that he now no longer had feet. He kicked with a barbed, like a dragon's tail.

Robyn looked on in amazement as Marion's new water vampire tail sent the bull shark scurrying away from him. Marion quickly whipped his barbed tail into the side of the bull shark approaching Robyn, too. "Must be from the second feather," he said in astonishment.

"Must be," an amazed Robyn said. "Let's get to the island 'fish boy' before anymore sharks head our way."

"Maybe we should head back to the seawall instead, even though it's farther away…I mean, now that I can swim faster with this water vampire tail?" Marion asked.

"Yeah, I was thinking the same thing, but now that you have a tail and gills, Marion, maybe we should head to Castle Pinckney to ask those water vampires exactly how to get you back to being human again. And, maybe the coast guard will spot us on the island? Maybe we could arrange the oyster shells into a 'HELP US' sign?"

"Good points," Marion agreed, "Let's head towards the island then before human scientists get their hands on me--I don't want to be experimented on as an 'alien fish boy' or something."

At that Robyn smiled, and they swam quickly towards the island which housed Castle Pinckney.

CHAPTER NINE

Magical Metal

Raven's metal had started vibrating back and forth between the bones in his arm from the moment he saw Robyn and Marion climb onto the shore of Shutes' Island. His metal generally acted that way only when it was spurring him onto action, or if it approved of something he'd accomplished (in that case it would move and grow longer and sometimes more ornate). Raven looked at Eric and then at Sirenetta. He noticed that their metals were moving now, too. "What are they telling us to do?" he asked out loud.

"I don't think our metals are telling us to attack them," Sirenetta said slowly, having learned the lesson from her metal after attacking Marion in the water earlier.

"Surely our metals can't be telling us to *help* them, right?" Eric questioned, truly perplexed.

"I don't know," Raven truthfully answered. "Maybe we have to now, to help Sirenetta get better." He'd been unsuccessful in spearing a fish for her to drain, as he was truthfully a little tired himself, so he looked for easier prey and found it. He first found a large male blue crab hiding under one of the rocks in the water, and Sirenetta gratefully bit into it by turning it stomach side up and then sinking her three beak-like fangs into it till it was completely drained of blood. The blood seemed to revive her a bit, but not nearly as much as the bright blue blood of the horseshoe crab he later found for her. She actually managed a smile after draining that one, so Raven knew she was feeling somewhat better.

Sirenetta felt her mind growing less cloudy, thanks to the crabs' blood now pumping through her. "Yes, I feel sure now that my metal is 'telling' me to help the humans for some reason. Maybe they hold the answer to how I can heal."

"I guess," Eric said slowly, annoyed that Raven had thought to get blood for Sirenetta and not him.

Expecting another battle with all three of the water vampires when they made it to the rocky shore of Shutes' Folly Island, Robyn planned to use another little known 'talent' of hers, as the Psychic Vampire Human she was. She planned on seeing if she could successfully scramble the thoughts of the three water vampires. Fully expecting to battle them mentally, she locked 'mental horns' with the female water vampire first, and surprisingly heard the thought telepathically relayed to her, *"We wish you no harm now...I think we can all work together to figure this **situation** out."* Robyn didn't know whether to be more shocked at the fact that the female water vampire was now being friendly, or to be shocked that they could obviously communicate telepathically, too, or at least it seemed. Robyn wasn't 100% sure that she was thinking correctly herself. Lots of things could have scrambled her own thoughts: water vampires, being followed by predatory sharks, the fact they were lying on the sand next to an old castle fortification and, last but certainly not least, the fact that Marion had kissed her twice, and was about to a third time (when they were interrupted by a 'little inconvenience' in the form of a shark!).

Water vampires could sometimes communicate telepathically with each other, but it was generally while underwater while they were hunting prey, and Sirenetta looked at the human girl with more fascination realizing that she could communicate her feelings/thoughts their way, the water vampire one, as well. Perhaps there was more to these human creatures than she'd heard tell. She knew of other vampires, powerful ones like Setiana, who walked on the earth above the water, and she'd always heard to be more concerned with them perhaps wanting her feathers—for one thing, if that kind, or even regular water vampires, were to get the last feather at the nape of her neck, they would probably be able to roam freely in the sun's rays, as long as they carried it. But, all that Sirenetta really knew about the feathers and their powers was really just hearsay, until that day, and she certainly didn't think human children, about her age, wielded much power. Clearly these two humans were proving her notions incorrect!

"Can you hear my thoughts?" was the first thing a very surprised Robyn directed to Sirenetta, after brushing off the sand from her arms and legs and wringing out her long dark hair.

"Yes," Sirenetta simply said.

"We can generally hear each other underwater without actually speaking aloud, for obvious reasons," Raven volunteered next.

"Yeah, I guess that makes sense," Marion added to the conversation.

Scowling at Marion, Eric growled, "Not that we generally share *our ways* with humans." He was thinking *with **mere** humans,* but he didn't say that out loud, after Sirenetta'd glanced over at him sharply when he started his talking with a growl.

Looking at Sirenetta, Robyn offered, "So we know what kind of perilous *situation* we're in with big predatory sharks who want to eat us out there, but what kind of *situation* are you in? Exactly? I mean, I realize you've lost your feathers, but what does that mean for you?"

"I'm weaker without them...at least while he's still holding them," Sirenetta offered, looking at Marion.

"And, why would I want to give them back to you? With them, I can breathe underwater and obviously swim faster and with more protection," Marion countered, looking at his new strong barbed water vampire tail, now flapped up on the shore of Shutes Folly Island–safely away from the sharks.

Angry that the humans hadn't immediately just capitulated to their will, Eric said, "Because you might not want to stay that way all your life...you'd have no home among our kind...it's a closed society, for all intents and purposes."

"Point taken," Marion smiled, "and who said I'd want to be a part of it anyway?"

Seeing that Eric's angry outburst was getting their negotiations nowhere, Raven piped in with, "I've got an idea...what if we helped you back to the Battery? Would you give Sirenetta her feathers back then?" Raven was thinking that IF they could convince these gifted humans to go back to their promenade walkway with their own water vampire escort, then there might be just enough time to get them there safely before sundown–before the adult regular water vampires awoke! That way, they'd never have to know about anything that transpired earlier in the day, and Sirenetta could just make sure her hair was always covering the nape of her neck, so that nobody else would realize she was missing two feathers. Though none of the young sol water vampires on Shutes Island were even sure that giving Sirenetta back her feathers would even help her regain her sol water vampire traits, they had to try something. Or maybe if they could just convince Marion to drop them, then that might do the trick. They just weren't certain, as it was something that was NOT taught at their Fort Moultrie Preparatory School for Water Vampires.

"What do you think, Robyn? Should we trust them?"

"I don't think we have a real choice," she said matter-of-factly. "Not if you're to stand a chance of your quality of life as you knew it remaining the same."

"It was a pretty good 'quality of life,'" Marion admitted with a broad smile, "so let's hope they'll honor their word as we will ours." And, with that he looked at Sirenetta, Raven and Eric—each directly in their eyes—before turning back towards the water.

"Wait a minute...let's talk logistics for just a minute," Raven said, as the word of reason. "Shouldn't we vamps be kind of surrounding you two on the way back? I mean, we've got our metal, and I don't see that you have any weapons—besides him having a barbed tail now," he offered, looking at Marion's new scaly barbed appendage.

"That's true," Robyn agreed, "plus, he's shark bait with his bleeding hand." At that reference, 'shark bait,' the three sol water vampires smiled, showing their peculiar beak-like fangs pierced through their upper gumline. They'd never heard of humans referring to themselves as food, so they thought that kind of cool and very funny in a very truth-be-told kind of way. "I'll go first, as I don't want to be behind that barbed tail Marion's sportin' now!" Robyn continued. At which the sol water vampires breathed in and out air so rapidly with strange sounds emitting from their mouths that Robyn and Marion were convinced they were either laughing very strangely or about to die from some strange kind of suffocation. Fortunately for their protective convoy-to-be, it was the former!

With Robyn in the lead, flanked by Raven on her left a little back and Eric on her right a little back (so that they could support Sirenetta on each side with her arms looped over their shoulders) and Marion with his new fierce tail protecting the rear, they all felt fairly confident that they could ward off any sharks along the 1.3 miles back to the seawall. One bull shark did dare to approach on the left, near Raven, but he successfully prodded it with his metal and sent it on its way with no meal for him in their literally tight knit group now. Raven was happy to feel his metal vibrate a bit afterwards and when he looked down a new symbol, it looked almost like a rose with thorns growing around it, had formed at the end of his metal. Obviously, his metal approved of him helping both the humans and his fellow sol water vampires out. His metal never ceased to amaze him, growing over what he hadn't even considered, when things he thought would spur it on to growth, like the strange metal object (camera) he'd gone for earlier, did nothing for it. Magical metal definitely had a mind of its own!

CHAPTER TEN

Low Battery

Jonas Lucas and his wife, Vanna Dittmar, were running low on energy, and as their unethical sort of psychic vampire had no problem draining from unsuspecting victims, they decided to go and get a quick fix from Jonas' own sister, Leticia, and her baby, Sean. They generally stopped by after going to their church service every week. But, Baby Sean had other ideas that week, as he realized that his Uncle and Aunt were on his way, and he didn't want to be drained of his energy again—like his evil uncle and aunt had done upon many occasions, but generally after their weekly church service. Yet, this week was also different because Baby Sean could intuitively feel that his sister, Robyn, was in real danger—more than just in having her energy drained by some ruthless Psychic Vampires in the family. So, Baby Sean decided to take things into his own very small, but very capable hands, by repeating out loud to his mother, "Rob-yn, Rob-yn, Rob-yn..." till she finally had to stop what she was doing—gathering more of her roses—and thorns.

"Are you telling me something about Robyn?" Leticia asked. "Do we need to go help her or something?" She was feeling particularly energized after ingesting her own blood again, thanks to a few thorn pricks to her fingers.

Happily noting that his mother was now less-than lethargic, Baby Sean bobbed his head up and down in a yes motion. Then he shouted "Rob-yn!" another time. That's all it took, as Leticia quickly scooped up her baby into her arms and headed to Murray Blvd. and Marion's house—where Robyn was supposed to be a birthday party guest. By the time Jonas and Vanna arrived at Leticia's house, there was no family to be found. The only thing they saw was a note Leticia had taped to the door in case they came by:

Gone to get Robyn from the Simons' house on Murray Blvd.–
Birthday Party!

Leticia

Not put off that easily, as they were really craving their
'human energy meal,' Jonas and Vanna decided to go to the
birthday party, too–even though they were NOT invited guests!

Will Lamely wasn't sure what was happening, but he was sure
he'd seen Robyn jump over the rails of Low Battery, near the stairs
leading to High Battery. So, he decided to go to the exact spot she
was at when he'd seen her jump. He thought he saw her dive into
the water, too, but he just couldn't be sure. When he got to the very
spot, at the railings where she'd jumped, and looked out at the
water, he saw nothing at first. Then, he thought he saw two heads
bobbing up and down, maybe three, he couldn't be sure. Then, he
had climbed the stairs to High Battery to have a better vantage
point, and then he was truly horrified by what he saw. He saw
shark fins headed towards the bobbing heads, and he couldn't be
sure, but he thought they were bull sharks. He thought briefly
about going in the water to help his crush, Robyn, but thought
better of it the next moment. He was a coward, but he told himself
that it would be more prudent to go and get help back at the
birthday party.

When Lamely arrived back at the party, many of the costumed
party guests had already left. He saw Mr. Simons standing near
the remains of the birthday cake with a worried look on his face.
Seeing that Wil Lamely had returned after being gone for some
time, he asked, "Have you seen my son?"

"Yes, he's...with Robyn," Lamely truthfully answered.

"Where?" Mr. Simons queried, with the concern not even veiled
in his voice.

"In the water."

"The water? Do you mean they've gone to somebody's pool
without letting me know?"

"No, sir, they're in the Charleston Harbor–that water–off of
Low Battery!"

"Wh—," Mr. Simons began, "nevermind, just show me where
you saw them." And, right as they were exiting his house, Leticia
and Baby Sean were about to enter. "Oh, Leticia...you'd best follow
me...your Robyn and my Marion...they're in trouble I think...in
the Charleston Harbor."

"In the water?" Leticia asked, but she already knew the answer, and so did her Baby Sean. "I'll follow you," she said grimly, holding tight to Baby Sean.

Molly and Candace were some of the few party guests remaining, as they wanted to say their goodbyes to Robyn and Marion before leaving but they figured that wasn't going to happen as they were nowhere to be found, so they'd planned on just making their exit and seeing them both at school soon to catch up. They were more than a little surprised and concerned after hearing the conversation between Mr. Simons and Ms. Lucas at the door. So, they quickly piped up, almost in unison, "How can we help?"

"Thanks for asking girls, just stay here, and keep an eye on things, okay?" They didn't really know exactly what they were supposed to keep an eye on, but they took it to mean that they couldn't leave the birthday party house anytime soon.

By the time Jonas Lucas and his wife, Vanna Dittmar, had arrived at the birthday party on Murray Blvd., it was just Candace and Molly there still keeping 'an eye on things' by just remaining there. "Wh-wh-where is everybody?" Jonas stuttered demandingly.

"Most birthday guests have already gone, and the others have headed down to Low Battery."

"Why?" Vanna Dittmar snapped.

"Robyn and Marion could be in trouble."

"H-h-how?" Jonas questioned authoritatively.

"We're not sure," Molly said softly, looking to her girlfriend for both confirmation and support.

"Try somewhere in the Charleston Harbor," Candace boldly offered next, as she didn't exactly appreciate the tone of Vanna and Jonas' voices, then she added as a more polite afterthought, "not to be rude, but we really don't know."

Vanna and Jonas looked at each other with hunger in their eyes, and before Candace and Molly knew exactly what had hit them, they were slouched in sleep by the doorway. Not having their 'regular family meal,' at least till they caught up with Robyn, Leticia and Baby Sean, they decided to take some 'fast food' elsewhere—in the form of draining the energy of Molly and Candace. Molly and Candace were no longer keeping an eye on things, but they weren't exactly suffering either, as they were both dreaming of the time they'd first kissed. Vanna and Jonas thought about draining the fat kid eating cake, too, but they decided there'd be better energy to be had with draining their family members, as those they preferred were of the Psychic Vampire Variety. Unfortunately, unscrupulous Psychic Vampires were known to sometimes drain the scrupulous Psychic Vampires.

So, that only left Lamely to keep an eye on things, but he didn't mind, as he'd much rather have the remnants of the birthday cake and other food to himself in the safety of a house on dry land away from sharks! And, he had absolutely no idea that he'd been spared being drained of his energy by two Psychic Vampires: Jonas and Vanna. He happily munched on the food and marveled at how tired Candace and Molly must've been to fall asleep at the front door while he waited on his ride.

Anxiously looking out into the water of Charleston Harbor, Leticia saw the strange convoy approaching first. She could see her daughter swimming in the lead, followed with two strange-looking boys not wearing shirts on either side of her, but a bit behind. She couldn't make out the two forms directly behind Robyn, but she assumed they were both human. She was, of course, wrong. She considered what to do next since she was holding Baby Sean in her arms and didn't want to let him down that close to the rails, which he could have easily crawled under and fallen to the sand and water below. Looking on beside her now with their children and company getting closer to them by the second, Andrew Simons exclaimed, "Is that Robyn with my son and three other kids in the water? What in the world..." he began.

"I don't know," Leticia interrupted, "but I have to help my daughter. Can you hold my son?"

"I've got a better idea. You stay here and watch your baby while I go down there." And, without wasting another second, Andrew kicked off his loafers and straddled the bars of low battery before jumping to the sandbar below. "Marion...Robyn...are y'all okay?" he asked, before diving into the water. He was about twenty yards away from the youthful convoy before he realized that only two in the group were human: his son, for the most part anyway, and Robyn. "What in the world..." he began to say again in a span of less than five minutes.

"Dad," Marion started, "no time to explain much, but these are our new *friends,*" he decided to say. "The girl is sick, and she needs our help. When we get to shore I'll explain more."

"Your hand, it's bleeding son," Mr. Simons said, anxiously looking around the water for any signs of sharks.

"I know," Marion said, "don't worry now, we've had some pretty awesome protection, for the most part." He then admitted, looking at Raven and Eric with some admiration.

"Okay, well you can tell me all about it later–when we're all safely on shore," Mr. Simons said prudently.

"Robyn, are you okay?" Leticia called from the rails at Low Battery when her daughter was safely on shore, while Baby Sean just smiled down at his sister.

"Fine, mom" Robyn responded. "We just made some new acquaintances is all."

"Really, *in* the Charleston Harbor?" Leticia quizzed, raising an eyebrow at the strange creatures who'd come on shore with her daughter. She had a feeling that whomever the boys and girl were–all with no shirts on, though Sirenetta's long hair covered her front–those weren't their Halloween-Birthday Bash Costumes. In fact, Leticia had a feeling that they hadn't even been invited to Marion's birthday party. And, of course, she was right!

The next moment, Leticia was unpleasantly surprised to hear a familiar voice to her right with, "H-h-hey Leticia, what are you doin' down here at Low Battery?"

"Don't worry, Jonas, just getting Robyn...she's been busy making new *friends,*" she said staring down at the three sol water vampires, hoping somehow that her brother wouldn't notice that fact.

But she wasn't so lucky, as Jonas stared down and exclaimed, "Wh-wh-what are they?"

"Costumes," Leticia quickly answered. "Some water show going on today, too. They're synchronized swimmers, of course." Not really caring about the energy meals in the water, due to their being too hard to get to, Jonas took that opportunity to lean in closer to his sister and started to drain the energy from her body. Leticia became so weak that she almost dropped Baby Sean, but Vanna was right there to snatch him away from her. Vanna intended to dine on his sweet baby energy, but Baby Sean had other ideas! Looking down at Robyn, he squirmed free from Vanna's clutches before she had an opportunity to drain his energy, and he quickly rolled under the bars of Low Battery– towards the sand below. But instead of meeting with the sandbar, his older sister, Robyn, was there to catch him.

"Baby Sean," was all Robyn said, happy to have him in her arms and away from both Vanna and Jonas.

Not happy to have lost her meal, Vanna decided that she too would jump down to the sandbar, where she intended to drain both Baby Sean and Robyn for her efforts. Meanwhile, Marion was about to say goodbye to his new water vampire friends, handing Sirenetta her feathers back. Almost immediately his gills disappeared, along with his barbed dragon-fish tail. And, Sirenetta almost felt as good as before her feathers were plucked. Almost. She was still hungry, though...she'd need more blood than just that of the two crabs to fully recover. She needed something big, but not something she cared for, as she'd come to care for the humans, Robyn and Marion. Seeing what had transpired between Vanna Dittmar and Robyn, plus reading the malintent in the older human's thoughts, Sirenetta looked at Robyn for her approval. Robyn just shook her head up and down once in acknowledgement and the okay for Sirenetta to take action. And, with a sudden propelling of herself forward, Sirenetta grabbed Vanna Dittmar by the arm, but before she yanked her into the water, she threw something Robyn's way with a "Heads up, human!" Robyn caught her silver bracelet with a smile. Then, Sirenetta quickly swam far from the sandbar with her new human prey, and then she dived deep into the waters of Charleston Harbor with her. Vanna Dittmar was sure that she'd drown in the deep waters, but she was wrong. Sirenetta intended to fully drain her of her blood long before she had the opportunity to drown, so that is exactly what she did. After years of draining the energy of those unwitting victims around her, it was truly a kind of poetic justice that Vanna Dittmar ended up being drained, too. Not even considering how her 'metal' would feel about her recent human meal of Vanna Dittmar, Sirenetta decided to surface to check on Raven and Eric. It was almost dusk, so the regular water vampires would be waking up soon. All the sudden, Sirenetta felt the metal in her hand move and then make a pleasant humming noise. She'd never heard it make that sound before, and looking down at it, she noticed it growing right before her very eyes with one of the most beautiful designs in the shape of a heart that she'd ever seen. Evidently, her metal had greatly approved of her killing Vanna Dittmar—and maybe her giving back the silver bracelet to the human girl, too!

Seeing Sirenetta's head pierce the water's surface, Jonas decided he'd jump down to the sandbar, too, while he shouted, "H-h-hey, what'd you do with my wife?" He easily jumped down to the sand, after having fed on his sister's energy. But there he was met with the glares of Robyn, Marion, Raven and Eric–even Baby Sean was glaring at him. Everyone except Mr. Simons, who still didn't really understand what was happening.

"Your wife is in 'the drink,'" Raven said, pointing to the waters of Charleston Harbor.

"D-d-doing what?" Jonas asked, with some fear creeping into his voice.

And, looking at both Robyn and Marion for the okay, which they both silently gave with a nod of their heads, as both Raven and Eric could telepathically 'read' Jonas' ill-intent, they each grabbed one of Jonas' arms and took him 'with them' into the deep waters of Charleston Harbor. But before they submerged with him some fifty yards out, they answered his question, "She was getting drained, of course, and you, are next!"

Raven and Eric shared Jonas' blood underwater, not realizing how depleted their own energy had become in the day's crazy events, but a full-grown human was just what the doctor ordered to restore their energy and overall health. Plus, much as Sirenetta's had done, their metal started growing and 'singing' to them almost immediately afterwards. They weren't looking for that reward of having their metal grow, but that's exactly what they got. And, therein lay the secret to many a mystery surrounding getting one's metal to grow: metals didn't like to grow when it was expected of them. Plus, true bravery and draining the bad guys and gals really scored points with the evolved metal. But, those lessons regarding one's metal weren't taught at their Fort Moultrie Preparatory School for Water Vampires–-no, those lessons had to be learned out in real life experiences!

Looking at all that had just transpired before his very eyes, Mr. Simons took action next by saying, "Look, let's all go back to my house. I'll put in a call to the coast guard and see if they can find your uncle and aunt, Robyn, and...and, we'll all sit down to discuss exactly what happened here today. For now, I'm just happy you're safe, son, and let's get that hand of yours bandaged up soon. Swimming in the Charleston Harbor with a bloody hand...really, son?" Mr. Simons half-way asked, tousling his son's blond curls.

"Yes," Leticia said slowly, looking at her daughter and her baby, "I suppose the coast guard should be called, though I'm not sure they'll believe what I think we all saw."

"What I saw," Mr. Simons said carefully, beginning to catch on after hearing Leticia speak, "was a married couple decide to foolishly swim out to the shark-infested waters of Charleston Harbor."

"Me, too," Robyn chimed in.

"Me, three," Marion agreed.

"Me, four," Leticia said with a smile.

'Me, fivah" Baby Sean added, surprising them all with his input.

And, that's exactly what they told the Coast Guard when questioned about it later. Even later, the bodies of Jonas and Vanna surfaced with their official death certificates reading something like 'Death by exsanguination–probable shark attacks.'

The 'incident' only brought Marion and Robyn closer together, and before long, they were as much of a known truly 'in love' couple as Candace and Molly were at their school. And, the 'coupling' didn't end there, as Leticia and Andrew finally decided to start seeing each other, too. Love was definitely in the air in Charleston, but not just 'in the air' as Raven and Sirenetta had started going out on long underwater daytime dates, with their parents' permission this time. And, Eric took the news pretty much in underwater water vampire 'swoosh' as he'd recently become enamored with a regular water vampire named Annacasea. He thought so highly of her that he'd even started sleeping during the day like the regular water vampires just so that he could be with her at night!

Wil Lamely didn't fare as well in the love department, but he didn't mind so much as long as he had his love affair with food to tide him over.

EPILOGUE

Vasario was practically dragging Setiana up the hill. Dawn was so near that Setiana would have no choice but to spend the day under a mound of dirt. They had nowhere else to go for the day. She was literally going to have to take a 'dirt nap.' And, that prospect was not looking at all good to her. She was tired of running from the light, tired of not putting down roots and even tired of Vasario always expecting her to be alright with their lots in life. But this time, she was not at all alright with their plight, and she was tired! Tired of the scrambling, the running, the very monotony of their type of existence. But Vasario was persistent with, "Setiana, you simply must get up this hill to the safety of a mound to sleep under!"

"No, Vasario, not this time. I 'simply must' listen to my own heart this time which is telling me that it's tired of running, tired of this existence!"

"Setiana, I cannot live without you!" Vasario pleaded.

Setiana stopped midway up the hill and turned to him, "It could have been different, Vassy, maybe if those children from the other time had come through for us even."

"Yes, well, My Love, we've never been able to count on anyone or anything but our own love."

"Yes, that's true, My Love," she agreed.

"And, now, you're quitting on our love?" Vasario asked, heartbroken.

"Seriously, Vassy, after NOT quitting on our love for centuries you ask me that? It's unfair. It's not our love, I'm just tired of running. Let the sun shine on my face and turn me to ash, I'm not running anymore!" Setiana exclaimed vehemently.

"Well, then, my life is over, too, because I do NOT want to live without YOU!" Vasario admitted with defeat in his voice.

"I'm sorry, My Love, but no more of this," Setiana said, picking up the dirt in her hand. "I won't ever sleep in this again!"

"Then sit with me here on the side of this hill, and let me embrace you as the sun rises," Vasario reasoned with Setiana.

"Alright, My Love," Setiana agreed, sitting down beside him. They watched in awe together as minutes later the sun kissed the hilltop and spilled down to where they were sitting in each other's embrace.

"Kiss me," Vasario said, and their lips locked in a love that was centuries old. Setiana expected to feel the pain of the rays of sunlight turning her flesh to ash next, but she felt nothing but the warmth of the sun's rays against her cheek and slightly flushed from Vasario's passionate kiss.

"Why am I not disintegrating?" Setiana asked, looking down at the sunlight on her hands and dress.

"I don't know," Vasario answered honestly. "Perhaps those children we were able to visit in their dreams came through for us after all–and showed without a question of doubt true love for each other through their selflessness and bravery–through time and space, somehow."

Indeed, and as was the way with much magic, its greatest feats occurred when least expected.

About the Author

G.L. Giles had hundreds of signings at most major chain bookstores and many wonderful independent bookstores in the Southeast and Midwest over the last several years. She's been on television 9 times talking about her books—on various stations in South Carolina, Georgia, and Alabama—and in 2008 she was interviewed by the legendary Joe Franklin (on his Bloomberg Radio show). She's also not a stranger to YouTube at this point with one of the videos on her books at over 72,000 views.

In addition, Giles reviews for *Infernal Dreams* and both interviews and reviews for her WordPress blog: *The GL Giles Files*. Admittedly, both feline and canine crazy, yet determined to break the 'crazy cat lady' stereotype, Giles lives with her **handsome husband**, seven cats, and one 'pittie' in rural South Carolina.

Also from BlackWyrm...

DARK HALO

by Christopher Kokoski

A winged stranger appears during a violent lightning storm, chasing Landon Paddock out into the maddening night with his estranged 15-year old daughter.

As layer after layer of reality is dissolved by a series of violent encounters, the only way to survive might be for Landon to band together with the family he destroyed to make one last stand against a sinister army of unthinkable magnitude.
[Supernatural Horror, ages 14+]

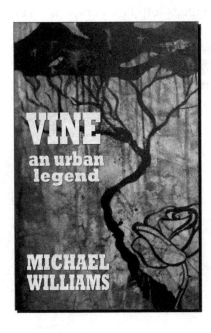

VINE

an urban legend

by Michael Williams

An amateur theatre director's sensational production starring an eccentric fly-by-night cast and crew draws the attention of ancient and powerful forces. Vine weds Greek tragedy and urban legend with dangerous intoxication, as the drama rushes to its dark and inevitable conclusion.
[Modern Mythic Fiction, ages 14+]

www.BlackWyrm.com

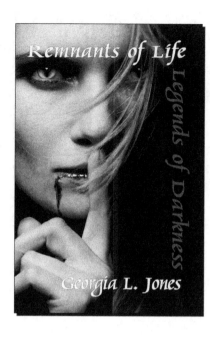

Remnants of Life: Legends of Darkness
by Georgia L. Jones

Samantha Garrett lives and dies a good life in the human world. She awakens a new creature, Samoda, a vampire-like warrior in the army of Nuem. She is forced to realize that she has become a part of a world that humans believe to be only "Legends of Darkness." Samoda finds her new life is entwined with the age old story of greed, love, betrayal, and vengeance.
[Urban Fantasy, ages 14+]

THE MAN IN THE BOX
by Andrew Toy

The box was his drug. It lulled him, cared for him and fulfilled his deepest desires... for a cost too high to pay.
　　Robbie Lake inadvertently climbs inside a cardboard box, which mentally transports him to a dangerous and mysterious island. He finds his identity in a secret world where he is hailed as a savior. The box quickly becomes his escape from reality.
[Fantasy Adventure, ages 14+]

AN UNFORGIVING LAND RELOADED

by Jason Walters

This collection of horrific short stories from Nevada's Black Rock Desert will give you nightmares for years to come. The very landscape of the desert it portrays seems to have a will of its own, as if possessed by a violent, hideous determination to purge all visitors from its bosom. It suffers only those few who need nothing.
[Horror Short Stories, ages 18+]

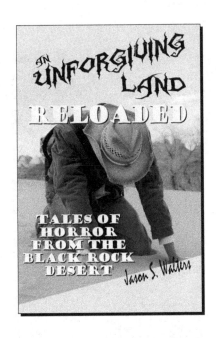

Burning the Middle Ground

by L. Andrew Cooper

This dark fantasy about small-town America transforms fears about the country's direction into a haunting tale of religious conspiracy and supernatural mind control. Burning the Middle Ground has as much appeal for dedicated fans of fantasy and horror as for mainstream readers looking for an exciting ride.
[Spiritual Horror, ages 14+]

CPSIA information can be obtained
at www.ICGtesting.com
Printed in the USA
BVHW041741041120
592505BV00011B/505